DEPENDING
ON YOU

ALSO BY MELISSA JAGEARS

UNEXPECTED BRIDES

Love by the Letter: A Novella

A Bride for Keeps

A Bride in Store

A Bride at Last

Blinded by Love: A Novella

TEAVILLE MORAL SOCIETY

Engaging the Competition: A Novella

A Heart Most Certain

A Love So True

Tied and True: A Novella

A Chance at Forever

FRONTIER VOWS

Romancing the Bride

Pretending to Wed

Depending on You: A Novella

NON-FICTION

Strengthen Your Fiction by Understanding Weasel Words

FRONTIER
VOWS

DEPENDING ON YOU

MELISSA JAGEARS

UTMOST
PUBLISHING
www.utmostpublishing.com

CHAPTER ONE

Wyoming Territory ~ December 1884

He hadn't expected a hero's welcome home, but neither had he anticipated a deserted street.

Bryant Whitsett dropped the oilskin back over the stage-coach's window. He couldn't tell whether his body was shaking more because of the cold, the stagecoach's awful springs, or the anticipation of seeing his wife, his eldest daughter, and the grandchild he'd yet to meet. He tugged his coat lapels higher and puffed warm air into his hands. Though he'd called himself a fool several times on the trip home for not buying a better coat, he'd wanted to keep every dollar he could to hand over to his wife.

Not that money would make up for anything he'd done to Leah—but surely it'd help some, considering how he'd left her to fend for herself for seven long months.

Four weeks ago, he'd been released from the Wyoming Terri-torial Prison with little more than the clothes he'd arrived in, which were wholly unsuited for winter weather. Since writing home for money to travel was out of the question, he'd walked to the nearest town in search of work.

Not many of the townsfolk had been keen on hiring a

stranger—not surprising with the prison close by. It'd taken nearly a month to work enough odd jobs to pay his way home. His lack of employability had only confirmed what he had to tell his wife. Since everyone in Armelle knew of his crimes, they'd have to leave if he had any hope of supporting them.

The day of the trial, he'd figured staying would be impossible. Folks from all over the county had come to watch the mayor and his cohorts get sentenced for defrauding land owners, cattle rustling—and murder. Though Bryant had only abetted the others by fixing the county's ledgers in an attempt to keep his boss from revealing his gambling debts, the glares the townsfolk had given him made it clear he'd not be welcomed back.

The driver called his team to a stop, and Bryant braced himself for his return.

As soon as the stage quit moving, the vehicle rocked as the driver, Charles Volkmann, climbed down from his high perch.

Forging out into the bitter cold, Bryant groaned. His joints already ached from the long ride. "I hope you're heading home for the night."

Though the winter sun hung far above the horizon, it would sink quickly, dragging snow along with it, if his nose was correct. Hopefully Charles wouldn't notice no one awaited his return. Had Leah not gotten the letter detailing his arrival?

"*Ja*, I am happy to get home." The big man rubbed his hands together, speaking softly as was his wont. His German accent seemed to be fading some. "You, as well, I am certain."

The greeting that awaited Charles would surely be warmer than his own. "Has your mother-in-law settled in yet? She's from Georgia, right? How's she doing with the cold?"

Charles shrugged as he continued to chafe his hands together. "She has not been able to come. We needed her room for anozer baby."

How enthusiastically should he congratulate the man? His wife had been so excited about having her mother come live with them. "Another babe is wonderful. Boy or girl?"

The man shook his head. "Two months yet more to wait. Zis weather makes it hard to add on another room, not zat I have zee money to do so." He sighed, though it turned into a chuckle. "With how many children we've got, I may end up on zee roof so Mutter can get here."

Bryant frowned up at the hulk of a man, one of the hardest-working, mild-tempered men he knew. If Charles couldn't have the life he wanted, perhaps Bryant had been a fool to expect his wife awaiting him upon his return.

After only a moment's hesitation, he pulled his money clip from his pocket and gave Charles his every last dollar. He'd make up for the loss later. Fighting tooth and nail to hold onto his money was how he'd gotten into trouble to begin with.

Charles's brow crinkled as he glanced at the money and then to Bryant. "But you already paid."

Bryant held up his hands. "Keep it."

The man's eyes widened as he counted the money. "Zis is more than twice zee price."

"A tip for getting me safely to prison and back."

The man's chuckle puffed white air between them. "I never thought anyone would give me a tip for taking them to prison."

"Enjoy it. For you'll never get another tip from me for the same reason."

"I hope so, Mr. Whitsett."

Though the man had treated him cordially since he'd picked him up at the last stage stop, the fact that he only hoped Bryant wouldn't return to prison didn't bode well for him. No doubt the other townsfolk wouldn't be far behind in their suspicions. But could he blame them? "You wouldn't happen to need another driver to help you with the stage?"

"Driving a stagecoach is different from a vagon. But I am sorry. I have no hours to spare."

He should be happy Charles hadn't laughed in his face for asking, like countless others surely would. "If you hear of any work I can do, will you let me know?"

"Of course." Charles's voice held a smidgen of pity.

Picking up his satchel, Bryant gave the man a nod. "I won't keep you any longer."

Charles pulled his hat down farther, his frosty breath swept away by the wind. "Merry Christmas."

Bryant returned the greeting as cheerfully as he could, but he wasn't at all certain he could do enough in the next few weeks to deserve a happy Christmas. Though seeing his family again would be enough.

Turning toward home, he forced his frozen feet forward. He ought to walk quickly, to get the blood flowing, but every step caused his lungs to tighten. The last time he'd seen his wife, she'd been unconscious, her face battered and bruised because of an accident he was ultimately responsible for. He'd had no idea his boss's hoodlums would kidnap her in an effort to force him into continuing to aid them, but if he'd not gotten involved in the first place, she'd never have been hurt. Though she'd not awoken until after he'd been locked behind prison bars, he'd been informed she'd survived—but with a limp and damaged vocal cords.

His daughter's letters hadn't told him much beyond that, though he'd been immensely grateful she still found him worthy enough to write. Whenever loneliness had punched him in the gut, he'd held on to the hope of seeing his first grandchild. Lenora was evidently a sweet, yet fussy baby, with a mop of brown curls and sparkling green eyes.

His wife hadn't written him but two lonely letters. The first informed him she was recovering, and the other only answered his question about how Ava was handling motherhood. Was Leah worse off than Ava had described?

Spotting one of the older women in town passing the mercantile, Bryant pulled his hat down low. It wasn't Mrs. Tate, thank goodness, but he wouldn't risk his arrival being broadcast across town faster than a coyote could streak across the ridge.

Minutes later, he stepped upon the dirt of his own street.

The windows in his cozy, green house were dark, and no smoke rose from the chimney. Had Leah moved in with Ava and her husband? If his wife's recovery had taken a long time, that would make sense. But why wouldn't his daughter have mentioned that in her letters?

He headed back. Hopefully the streets would be as empty on his way to Ava's as they'd been on his way here. But before he turned off Main, a dark-haired, petite form wearing a green dress he recognized crossed the street toward the laundry. Heart hammering, he watched his wife stop in front of the town's laundress, who was wearing a green dress of her own. He'd never seen Corinne in anything but a white shirtwaist and dark skirt. When the tall blonde took leave of his wife and climbed into an awaiting wagon, his gaze stayed riveted on Leah, who'd turned to wave farewell.

How had he forgotten how lovely she was?

Barely breathing, he took one step, then another as he strode down the boardwalk on the opposite side of the street to close the distance between them.

What if she turned her back on him?

In prison, he'd longed for the day he could return home and hold her for days on end, despite not deserving such comfort.

Leah opened the laundry's door and limped through. Was she working for Corinne now?

Across the way, Leah flipped over the closed sign. Strange. Why was she closing the laundry and not Corinne?

The sign rocked to a halt only to swing again as Leah pushed backwards out the door, a wrapper tucked tightly around her. Without looking his way, she marched in the opposite direction, a limp slowing her progress. Wasn't she going home?

He clamped his lips to keep from calling after her. Best they have their first encounter away from the public eye. Her irregular movements matched the haphazard beat of his heart. He was going to have to have a talk with the doctor about the obvious pain she was in.

After crossing the street, he followed her, taking surreptitious glances, hoping no one called to him while he was basically stalking his wife.

At the bank, she reached for the door just as the bank president backed out, keys in hand.

"Mr. Rice." Leah stumbled backward.

"Oh!" The balding man startled and twisted to look behind him. "Mrs. Whitsett, I completely forgot."

"If now's not a good time…" Her voice no longer held the clear timber he remembered, but rather sounded more like harsh grit.

The bank owner opened the door wider and swung an arm to usher her in. "The time is yours. We can still sign the papers."

Papers?

And then they both disappeared into the bank.

Had she lost the house? With renewed energy, he bounded up the bank stairs. He had paid off the house. They couldn't lose it now that he was back, or at least not until they had a chance to sell it.

He pulled hard on the door, breathing easier when he found it unlocked. "Mr. Rice," he called. "Please, wait!"

Bryant stopped midstride at the wide-eyed, almost fearful expression on Leah's face. He'd hoped to have her crash into his arms the moment he returned, but the look she gave him was definitely not longing.

"Um, I'm sorry to barge in." He nodded at her slightly before addressing Mr. Rice. "But please, give us an extension so I can pay whatever we owe before you take the house."

Mr. Rice glanced between them. "I'm sorry, I don't under—"

"I'm not selling the house, Bryant." His wife's gravelly tone was less from cord damage and more from a hostility he'd never heard her direct at anyone. "It's not in danger. I'm buying the laundry."

"The laundry?" He turned toward Mr. Rice. "She can't buy that."

Leah straightened all five foot two of her. "Don't you dare, Bryant. You don't know—"

"But that will only complicate things since…well. We need to talk about this outside of Mr. Rice's presence." He knew he hadn't flat out told her in his letters they couldn't stay in Armelle, hoping to let her adjust to the idea, but she couldn't have missed his worries in that regard. Unless of course, she'd thrown his letters straight into the fire—if that was the case, employment was the least of his worries.

Mr. Rice cleared his throat. "Uh, well, perhaps today is not the day to put this into writing."

She whipped back toward him. "It is. It's the day we arranged to do it."

"But you don't have your husband's permission."

Leaning across the counter, she tapped on the papers. "I didn't need his permission while he was gone, and I've done everything you've asked."

Tugging on his tie, Mr. Rice pulled the paper gently out from beneath Leah's fingers. "I don't know if…well, I'm going to need some time to be sure the bank can—"

She huffed. "Fine, I'll keep renting."

"I'm afraid your lease is up at the end of the year."

"What?" Her shoulders drooped. "You mean you won't renew the lease?"

Mr. Rice glanced toward him, and Bryant shook his head slightly.

Leah turned fast enough to see him do so. She glared at him then stomped past, leaving him in a wake of the scent of her favorite lavender shampoo. His heart clenched, but he clamped his hand around the counter's edge to keep from chasing after her.

Her expression had been hard. Real hard.

He was thankful she wasn't blanketing him with the kisses and praises he'd never deserved, but for her to have uttered such harshness in public? It wasn't like the Leah he remembered—not at all.

The bank door slammed behind her, and the windows rattled, reverberating through the empty hollows within him.

Those first few days, when her life had teetered on the brink of death, he'd told God he'd accept living separated from her if he must—if only God would save her life. He'd done plenty to deserve such a punishment.

But after spending only a few seconds in her presence...

Lord, I lied to you. She might be better off without me, but there's no way I can live without her.

Leah marched back to the laundry. How dare Bryant show up at the bank and ruin another part of her life.

Her hip ached, especially with the cold, but she kept her boots thumping against the boardwalk. She needed to put more distance between herself and Mr. Rice, who'd so easily rescinded his offer just because her husband had shaken his head no. Her husband, who'd helped the mayor defraud half the county last year! His say-so shouldn't have undone anything.

"Leah!"

Her heart clenched at Bryant's broken voice.

She swallowed hard but kept moving forward. He wasn't the only one who'd been broken.

"Wait!" He jogged up and stopped in front of her.

Seemed he'd stayed active in prison, his chest and arms were broader and more muscled than she remembered. Averting her gaze, she passed by him. "I can't believe you."

"About what?"

As if he didn't know. When he showed up, what did he do?

Apologize? Grovel? No. He'd made a life-altering decision without consulting her—which was exactly the reason they were in this mess to begin with. "You don't get to make financial decisions without my input ever again."

He stopped, but after a moment, his footsteps continued behind her. "But isn't that what you were doing? You didn't tell me anything about buying a laundry in the two letters you sent me."

She hugged herself as she recalled the scads of paper she'd written on only to crumple and toss them into the trash. Though writing the words that had festered inside of her had felt good, they'd been too harsh to send. "I think I've earned the ability to make decisions on my own now, considering we would've lost the house if I'd not taken over the laundry."

"How's that? It's paid off."

She whirled on him. "How was I supposed to maintain it or keep it warm without a cent in the bank? How was I supposed to feed myself? I can't eat furniture."

He pulled on his neckcloth. "I figured Oliver would help."

"He didn't deserve such a burden. Besides, he and Ava have enough to worry about without me piling my problems onto theirs."

"I understand I put you in an awful spot—"

She scoffed. "An awful spot wasn't the half of it."

"I know, and I'm sorry. But you can't buy the laundry. Not when we have to leave town."

She shook her head. When he'd hinted to that in his letters, she'd stopped writing him. "Our first and only grandchild is here."

"I don't want to leave either, but haven't you read any of my letters? I don't think we have much choice. Who's going to hire me here after what I've done?"

"You should've thought about that before you swindled people." She stomped around him and pulled out her keys to the laundry.

"What if we moved closer to Jennie?"

She paused, swallowing hard. Finding him a job in Chicago would certainly be easier, but Jennie was content at the blind school. "She doesn't need us like Ava does. You'll just have to find something here, because I'm not leaving."

Bryant's brow was deeply furled.

She let out a long, frosty breath. She'd never before talked to him so sharply or told him no so adamantly. But whereas she used to think he hung the moon and the stars, every time she looked in the mirror now, she was reminded of how naïve she'd been.

She stopped herself from reaching up to touch the scar that ran through her eyebrow and jammed her keys into the lock. Busying herself with the door might just keep the warmth in the back of her eyes from becoming tears. Though he deserved the townsfolk's distrust, he wasn't the only one who'd messed up. Why had she not questioned him last year when she'd known something was wrong?

"I'm staying in the laundry's upstairs apartment," she said with a slight tremble in her voice. "You can have the house."

"I—"

When he didn't finish his sentence, she couldn't help but turn.

His face was paler than the winter sky. He looked down the road as if to be sure no one would overhear. "I figured I'd be sleeping in the guest room, but for us not to be together at all?"

Why she remained standing in the cold staring at him, she didn't know, but she couldn't turn her back on him when he looked like a puppy that'd been tossed off a stage.

Then he stepped closer, and the invisible thread that had stitched two hearts together pulled tight, nearly making her stagger with the desire to collapse into his arms and pretend last year had never happened. She looked away, her chest tightening with the effort to resist.

"What happens if I can't find a job here?" His voice was barely audible.

She crossed her arms, clamping against the ache. "Then you'll have to look harder—or somewhere else."

He pulled off his hat, his ears red with cold. "But how can I make things up to you if we're not together?"

Her throat constricted. "You likely can't."

"I know I don't deserve a second chance, but is there any love left in your heart that could convince you to extend me one? I'll work hard to make up for everything wrong I've ever done to you."

Tears welled hot against her frozen face.

He took another tentative step forward, holding out a gloved hand. "I can't do that if we're apart."

She took a step back and pushed against the door. "I'm not ready for that."

Once inside, she closed the door before he could say anything else. Over the last few months, she'd imagined the moment she'd show him exactly how little control he had over her now.

But no cathartic rush swept over her by shutting the door in his face.

She only felt more alone.

CHAPTER TWO

Leah half-heartedly stirred the beans on her daughter's stove top later that evening. She should've told Bryant he could eat dinner here, but this was likely the last hours she'd have before needing to decide what to do about him. Of course, she'd been trying to decide that for months. He'd been good to her for so many years, but then he'd failed her completely. How could she ever go back to trusting him as she had before? She'd never been one to hold grudges, but then, she'd never been so humiliated—and his secrets had nearly gotten her killed.

Besides, he'd never before insisted they do something she was so set against. How could she leave Ava?

She glanced over at her daughter, who was attempting to feed the baby before dinner. However, Lenora seemed more interested in massaging porridge into her curly hair than eating it. Ava's six-month-old had yet to meet her grandfather. Would Ava hand the baby over to Bryant as if he hadn't missed out on her entire life so far? Let Lenora get attached only for him to leave again?

With a sigh, Leah set down her spoon. Of course Ava would. There wasn't a man in this world who got a bigger sparkle in his eye when handed a baby than Bryant. When Ava was born, she'd fallen more in love with him watching him coo at their daughter as if she was the eighth wonder of the world.

But knowing he intended to leave almost made her wish he'd stayed away. He'd get Lenora enraptured with his silly voices, only to take his leave of her soon after—and Lenora's father wouldn't come near to making up for her grandfather's absence.

Leah slammed the lid back on the beans. How many hours were left until Bryant disrupted the comfortable routine they'd created without him? Did he really have to upend everything all over again?

And then there was the matter of her heart—its broken pieces cracked all the more at the mere thought of him leaving her behind.

"Oh, look at me." Ava groaned and swiped at the porridge on her bodice.

Leah grabbed a towel. "Here, let me get you a—"

Squealing, Lenora flung her spoon onto the floor.

Oliver, Ava's husband, walked in from the back hallway, hair wet from his bath. "Good evening, Mother." He leaned down giving the top of Ava's head a perfunctory kiss. "Darlin'."

Ava looked up at him. "Could you take Lenora and clean her up? I need to help Mama finish supper."

Oliver glanced at his daughter then shook his head. "Gotta bring in more wood."

"Why not after..." Her voice trailed off as she frowned at her husband's retreating back. "Oliver!"

He turned before closing the door. "Why not appreciate what I do? The baby won't melt wearing food, but she'll freeze without wood."

The door slammed, and Leah cringed. She wiped her hands on the towel. "Here, I can take her."

"No, it's even harder for you to work holding a baby than me." Ava took the towel and cleaned up her daughter's chubby arms. "Sorry about that. Last night, I got mad at him for refusing to be Joseph in the nativity. Then my resentment over

him ignoring Lenora spilled over, and I yelled more than necessary. I mean, he played with his nephew Ezekiel just fine two
years ago, even played peek-a-boo. I think he's ignoring her just
because she's a girl."

Leah had never seen Oliver hold anyone's baby, boy or girl,
but what did that have to do with the Christmas program? "He
said he wouldn't be Joseph?"

Ava's face hardened as she wiped off Lenora's cheeks.

"I'm sorry, honey." Her daughter had always been excited
for the day she'd be the mother to Armelle's youngest baby and
get to be Mary in the nativity with her husband playing Joseph.
Ava had also planned for her sister to sing as the angel, but of
course Jennie couldn't do that from Chicago. Another blow to
Ava's hopes.

Leah pressed a hand to her throat. She'd agreed to sing in
Jennie's place to keep Mrs. Tate from volunteering. That old
woman didn't need to be anywhere close to Ava and her family
while they were struggling. Though Mrs. Tate surely had good
intentions deep down inside her somewhere, they'd yet to mani-
fest themselves.

Unfortunately, singing meant the whole church would hear
the voice Leah no longer used if she could help it, and they'd
pity her all the more.

"Jesus is a girl, and Oliver won't be Joseph." Ava stood and
sighed, hugging Lenora to her chest, then moved to pull the
bread from the oven one-handed. "And my costume's only half
done, and I want to cry. People shouldn't feel like crying at
Christmas."

"Nursing made me just as weepy as when I was pregnant, so
maybe it's just that. But it's all right to cry. Better than bottling it
up." If only she could tell her daughter everything would be
fine, but her own worries would likely make such encourage-
ment sound flat.

Leah took the bread from Ava and shooed her from the
stove. "Who will you have stand in for Joseph?" She shook her

head. Of course, Bryant would. She should tell Ava her father was home. But then he'd come to rehearsals. And he'd hear how she sang, and he'd notice how her face was—

"Celia's going to be Joseph."

"What?" Leah jerked upright. "The sixteen-year-old with a chip on her shoulder?"

Ava smiled, the first one she'd sported since Leah had come to help with dinner. "What other Celia do you know?"

"She would actually do that? Stand up in front of church in a costume?"

"You've done a world of good for her, Mama."

"Not me, exactly." She touched the slack muscles weighing down her mouth in a permanent half frown. The day Celia had tried to rescue her from the rustlers the young lady had been in cahoots with had ended in disaster. Though if Bryant hadn't gotten mixed up with them in the first place, they'd never have kidnapped her in an attempt to force his hand. "What happened to me and the guilt she won't let go of…that's what changed the girl."

The back door banged open. Leah turned expecting to see Oliver, but Spencer, a curly-haired bundle of energy, ran in instead. "Mrs. Ronstandt! Guess what?"

Celia, his sister, tromped in after him, as if they'd been waiting around to hear her name before entering. She grabbed the door her brother had flung open and shut it gently. "Spence, you're going to put a hole in the wall one of these days."

The nine-year-old ignored his sister and bounced straight to Ava. "Pa said yes, Mrs. Ronstandt!"

"That's goo—"

"Spence, you need to settle down." Celia grabbed him by the shoulder as if to keep him on the floor.

"What's this all about?" Leah took in the mischievous gleam in the boy's wide eyes. After Spencer's mother, Annie, had remarried, this outgoing boy had turned up the notches on his ability to light up a room.

Ava put a hand on his head and mussed his auburn hair. "Spencer's going to—"

"Pa said I could be the angel." Spencer threw out his arms and twisted under Ava's hand like a top.

Leah swallowed, unable to look at her daughter. She knew her voice wasn't worth much, but—

"Don't worry, Mrs. Whitsett. You're still going to sing because I can't sing that high." Spencer took her right hand and patted it. "And you're too heavy to fly."

She peered down at him. "Fly?"

"Yeah! Mrs. Key is going to rig me up a harness and pulley, so Pa can hoist me clear to the rafters." He spread out his arms and zoomed around the kitchen table, much to Lenora's toothless, drooly grinned delight. "I'm going to fly!"

"But wouldn't Celia rather be the—"

"Celia's too heavy to fly." He bumped into a chair, but caught it before it clattered, then went back to buzzing around. "So that's why I have to be the angel."

The young lady crossed her arms over her nearly flat chest. "There's no way I'm hanging from the rafters trussed up like a bird."

"And that's why she's Joseph, so I can fly." He squawked, more like a distressed hawk than anything that'd emit from an angel.

She turned to Celia. "But Joseph isn't a girl—"

"And Jesus ain't a girl either, but he has to be this year." Spencer stopped in front of Ava and blew a playful buzz against Lenora's chubby arm.

Instead of giggling, the babe frowned so deeply she looked like a grumpy old man.

"I guess you have me there." Leah couldn't help her smile.

"Besides, Ma said angels are boys anyway. Who knows why they started using girls. You don't hear girl angel names in the Bible. So, I'm fine. And small. That's what's important."

She grinned at his enthusiasm. "And your father really agreed to hoist you up on a rope?"

Celia rolled her eyes. "Men are just big boys. Jacob insists I have to start making grown-up decisions, but I'm not the one who's been trying to out spit Spencer all week—when Ma ain't looking, of course."

Leah took in Celia's rigid form. "Are you all right with being Joseph?"

She shrugged. "It got me out of wearing a sparkly halo—which I have no right to wear."

"Hey, you two." Their mother popped in through the back door. Annie's rounded belly was just becoming discernible, but the near permanent smile on her face made the bigger impression.

It was so good to see her happy—even though now, Leah's own joy seemed as far away as Annie's had once been.

"You two shouldn't leave me in the dust." She blew a limp strand of red hair off her face. "I get winded easily these days."

"Mrs. Ronstandt said yes!" Spencer slammed into his mother's middle.

Annie cringed. "Oh, child, be careful."

He backed away, shoulders slumped. "Sorry, Mama."

Annie looked to Ava. "Did he actually ask you if it would be all right?"

Ava placed a hand on Annie's shoulder. "Not exactly. But I'm fine with him making the part his own." Though Ava was smiling, there was a touch of sadness on her face Annie likely wouldn't notice. "I'm fine with whatever he wants to do."

Which meant her daughter had given up on what she'd always hoped for.

"Great." Spencer's face lit even more. "I bet I can come up with even better stuff. You'll have the best nativity ever." The boy gave a quick peck to his mother's slightly swollen abdomen before zooming out the back door into the cold.

Ava watched him disappear with a blank expression. "Mrs.

Hendrix, what do you think about your family taking over this year's nativity?"

"What?" Leah stepped forward. "You've always wanted to do this."

She shrugged. "Maybe I should wait until I have a boy."

"But what if you always have girls?" Celia asked, from where she was leaning against the table.

The sadness on Ava's face made Leah want to punch Oliver in the nose. How dare he make her daughter worry about having more beautiful, healthy baby girls like Lenora. Leah placed a reassuring hand against Ava's back. "Oliver will adjust, if that happens."

She nodded meekly and readjusted Lenora, who was draped heavily upon her shoulder. "Of course. Excuse me, I'm going to put Lenora down. Though I hope she doesn't nap too long or I'm not going to get much sleep again tonight."

Considering the dark circles under her daughter's eyes, Leah doubted Oliver was helping at night, either.

Annie stepped closer to Leah as Ava headed to the back bedroom. "Are you sure she's fine with Spencer and Celia being in the nativity? I know my boy's excited to 'fly,' but if that's going to be a problem, I can explain it to him."

"I'm certain it's all right. She's just been overwhelmed lately."

"Let me know if she changes her mind." Annie squeezed Leah's shoulder. "And let us know when Bryant returns so we can have you both out to the ranch. Jacob is eager to have you over for dinner."

Probably because he knew how the town would likely shun his friend and was hoping to lead by example. If Jacob and Annie only knew how unsure she was of what to do with Bryant herself. "Thanks. He'll be happy to spend some time with Jacob, I'm certain."

Annie took her leave and Leah started setting out plates, trying hard not to think about how dinner with the Hendrixes would go if she hadn't the courage to have her husband over for dinner right now. Maybe she should stay behind and let him go on his own.

"What's wrong, Mother?"

Leah jumped at Ava's question. She turned to see her daughter watching her from the kitchen doorway. "What do you mean?"

"The cloud hanging over you seems darker today."

She put out another plate. "I'm just wondering what to do about your father."

"Papa?"

"I...Do you—oh, of course you do." She sighed, then nodded at Oliver who'd come in through the back door with an armful of wood. "What I mean is, I'm sure you want him to be here, but I couldn't ask him to—"

"You mean he's back?" At Leah's weak nod, Ava straightened to her full height. "Why didn't you tell me? Oliver, did we get a letter from Papa recently?"

"Not that I know of."

She faced Leah again. "Why isn't he here?"

Leah couldn't keep eye contact with her daughter. "I don't know where he is at the moment."

Oliver deposited his wood by the stove, and Ava sidled over to whisper, "What's wrong? Are you two having problems like Oliver and me?"

"Oh, honey." Leah smoothed back her hair, as if Ava wasn't a mother herself now. "Some days are hard, but we'll get through it." Hopefully.

Oliver stretched and yawned. "Is it time to eat yet?"

"Of course." Leah took out the ham, which had stayed warm in the oven.

Oliver rubbed his hands together as he sat in his chair. "You'd think I'd get used to the cold working outside all day, but every evening it seems to take me longer to get warm. At least the weather's not slowing me up like Smith. He really shouldn't be working the tracks anymore."

As Oliver related the mundane goings-on of the shipping yard, Leah remained silent.

How was she going to keep the bleakness she felt hidden from everyone? If Ava was beginning to see…well, it wasn't like she'd had reason to practice hiding dark emotions from her daughter before. But how was she going to help Ava if her own marriage was falling apart?

How many years had she looked forward to being the doting grandmother, the dispenser of wisdom, the type of mother-in-law a man would praise? Instead, she wasn't any one of those things. No one should take advice from a woman who'd so thoroughly misjudged her husband. But she'd not failed as a mother, so she needed to focus on that.

Lenora's quiet mewling interrupted Ava's description of the sad state of her Christmas costume. "Good, she's up already. Could you get her, Oliver?"

He wiped his mouth and pushed away his empty plate. "I thought you wanted me to fix the dresser drawer?"

"I do, but—"

"I can't do both." He quit the table and headed out the back door, leaving Ava to stare at her unfinished food.

Lenora cried again, and Ava stood.

"I'm full. Let me get her." Leah tossed her napkin onto the table. If anyone in this house needed to finish eating, it was Ava.

"No, Mother. I can do it."

Leah stood anyway and gently pushed Ava back toward her chair. "With babies, you need all the energy you can get. Don't refuse help when you've got it."

Ava sat and slammed her chin into her hand. "You're the only help I get."

Leah had to force herself not to glare out the backdoor window. "When Lenora's old enough to talk and do things, surely he'll take more of an interest. But if he doesn't, when your husband fails you in one area, you forge on." As she'd done with the laundry. "Meanwhile, shower this baby with twice the love until he comes around. We'll pray he does." She gave Ava's shoulders a quick rub, then left to retrieve Lenora, whose cries were growing more insistent.

Upon returning and after Ava had finished eating and taken the baby back, Leah shooed her daughter out of the room. She'd scour the kitchen spotless in hopes of lifting her girl's spirits.

Half an hour later, a knock sounded on the front door. Leah froze. Oliver wouldn't have knocked.

Ava called to the visitor to come in and then the door whined open.

"Oh, ho, ho there! Who is this?"

Ava emitted a lighthearted squeal, and then soft scuffling sounds—likely her daughter throwing herself into Bryant's arms —followed.

Leah's heart bottomed out. If only she could've run into his embrace with such joy. But she couldn't have—it would've been fake.

And yet, she nearly trembled at the thought of being where her daughter stood now.

"Hello, hello, baby." Bryant's voice cracked a bit. "You don't know who I am now, do you? We'll have to fix that."

Lenora's scared whimper almost broke Leah's heart.

"Honey, Grandpa isn't going to hurt you." Ava began shushing her.

"Don't worry about it, Ava. She'll get used to me in time. You keep her. Maybe it's my beard. Should Poppa shave it off? Or is Poppa what you call Oliver?"

"No." Ava's voice sounded strained.

"What's wrong, honey?"

Leah couldn't decipher Ava's muffled answer, likely from being pressed against her father's chest.

Rubbing her hands dry a second time, Leah took in a fortifying breath. Ava didn't need to deal with lost dreams, an unco-operative husband, and her parents giving each other the cold shoulder. She stepped through the kitchen doorway and swallowed hard at the sight of Bryant's arms tight around Ava while Lenora pulled on her mother's skirts from where she sat on the rug.

"There's ham I could heat up," she said, her heart stuck somewhere up in her throat.

Bryant peered over Ava's head, his eyes tinged red. "I've eaten," he answered with a rough warble. "I came to see Ava and the baby. But perhaps I could walk you home?"

Lenora's cries became more insistent as she toppled over. She was still having trouble sitting up on her huge diapered bottom.

Walk home with Bryant? Now? She wiped her clammy hands on her apron and looked at the clock. "I'm afraid I'm not leaving anytime soon. I was going to stay and help," she answered loudly over the baby's sobbing. Though little left needed doing, she could surely find—

"Excuse me." Ava stepped out of Bryant's arms and picked up Lenora. "I need to feed her."

Once Ava was out of earshot, Bryant frowned at her from across the room. "You don't want me to walk you home, do you?"

She shook her head. She'd have no idea what to do with herself. "Good night, Bryant." Turning, she walked back into the kitchen, then leaned heavily against the table.

Her heart was still pitter-pattering at seeing Ava snuggled up against Bryant. Was she jealous she couldn't be in his arms or miffed because Ava felt comfortable enough to cuddle up despite how he'd upended their whole world?

A minute later, Bryant appeared in the doorway. "Are you planning for us to talk only when absolutely necessary? Don't you think seven months apart is too much already?"

Her lungs faltered. How to explain that his imprisonment

had been as bad for her as it'd been for him? "You left me penniless and completely embarrassed, struggling to take care of myself. Prison time might have given the folks you took advantage of some semblance of justice, but it didn't help me any."

"I'm so sorry. I wish I could undo everything. But it's not like you to be… well, I'd rather you yell at me than not talk to me. We've got to figure things out together."

She nearly laughed envisioning herself yelling at him. Besides this morning, when had she ever really raised her voice at him? But the mountain between them wasn't funny. "For months, I thought I could have a good rail at you when you returned, but after talking to you the way I did earlier? It wasn't as satisfying as I'd hoped. But I don't feel like being nice to you either. I can't go back to how things were." Her throat clogged and she looked away from him.

"How can you be sure unless we try?"

She shook her head. It wasn't possible.

"What can I do to regain your trust? To get us back on good terms?"

"I wish I knew." Despite the strength she tried to instill into her words, her voice sounded as broken as she was. She clamped shaky hands around the table's edge. After a minute of silence, she looked over at him.

He swallowed hard, jaw tight. Half a year ago, seeing him fighting off tears would've been the worst thing in the world for her, but now, maybe he realized how much damage he'd caused —not to the town, but to her belief in him.

With a deep breath, he nodded and bent to pick up an abandoned spit-up rag Ava must've dropped. Wordlessly, he handed it to her, then turned, leaving the kitchen with a heavy tread.

She strangled the cloth in her hand. He'd likely not do her wrong again, but their relationship couldn't simply return to normal because he'd come back. He'd have to earn back her trust—if that was even possible—before she could go anywhere with him.

She dropped the rag into the hamper and headed toward Lenora's room. In light of Ava's exasperated sighs and the repetitive rhythm of drawers opening and closing, her daughter was likely searching for a new outfit for the baby.

Never had she thought the day would come where she'd not follow Bryant to the ends of the earth. But that time had come.

CHAPTER THREE

In the mercantile, Bryant pretended to be interested in shoe polish as he waited for a woman in a threadbare shawl to finish reading the advertisements on the cork board. Last year, he'd have asked her what kind of work she was looking for, but what good could he do her now? If she told anyone he'd recommended her for a position, she might be turned away. Once the woman left, just as slumped as she'd been before, he moved to the cork board, fearing he'd not have much luck either.

His heart sank with each notice he read. He'd already inquired after all these positions, even the ones he'd had no notion of how to do.

All but the top left advertisement anyway. Seemed the printer hadn't been truthful when he'd said he had no position open. The handwritten post indicated he'd put the notice up two days ago.

Rather than tear the paper off the board, Bryant breathed in deep and slow. Chris could've hired someone before he'd gotten there—and even if he hadn't, not wanting to hire a convicted criminal wasn't anything unusual. He'd spent all day listening to people explain why they couldn't hire him for paperwork—for which he was best qualified—and why it wouldn't be "good for business" to take him on for anything else.

He ambled over to the front window and puffed hot air against its frosty pane. The street was crowded despite the snow flurries, probably because of the incoming train. He rubbed his hands along his arms. Despite his age, surely he could keep up with an inexperienced laborer, but to work at the rail yard with Oliver? He wouldn't force his son-in-law to have to distance himself from his wife's father to safeguard his reputation.

Bryant looked to the other side of town where the ridge stood like a sentinel over the sweeping plains. He likely couldn't get hired on for ranch work, considering he'd been convicted of helping the former mayor steal land from numerous county ranchers.

The only job in desperate need of filling was that of marshal, and he wouldn't bother to apply for that. He'd have to keep trying for a labor job of some sort until he mended his reputation. Getting work with the railroad would probably be easiest, but he couldn't be away that long, not with the way things were between him and Leah.

He drummed his fingers against his bicep. How long would it take to earn back her confidence?

Maybe he should ask Jacob or Nolan if they could use him, even if that meant staying in the bunkhouse. Though it was too late to ride out now and ask. He'd interrupt their supper.

His stomach rumbled on cue, and he glanced at his pocket watch. Ava had invited him to dinner this evening, but Leah likely didn't want him to come. But after months of prison food, the canned beans he'd eaten every day since release had completely lost their charm—if they'd ever had any.

After waiting for the young family near the front door to move away, he slipped out of the mercantile. As had happened all week, the people on the boardwalk gave him a wide berth. Deputy Dent nodded his head as they passed, but his gaze was hard and measured.

Bryant turned down the alley. He'd take the long way to Ava's to avoid as many people as possible.

After knocking on his daughter's door, he turned the knob, unwilling to wait on the doorstep longer than necessary in the blustery weather. The trills of a well-tuned piano filled the room. "Hello?"

"Hey, Papa." Ava's voice called out over the Christmas song she was playing. He couldn't quite remember the name of it though, being one Ava had sent off for only last year.

After stepping inside and shutting out the wind, his stomach growled again. What smelled so good? He crossed the front room to peek into the kitchen despite his heart thumping over-time at the possibility of catching his wife unaware. But the kitchen was empty. He resisted the urge to check on what smelled like onions and beef for fear he'd be unable to resist eating straight from the pot.

Forcing himself away from the promise of a delicious dinner, he couldn't help but smile at Ava's off-key singing rising above the discordant baby babble.

He sat on the sofa to watch Ava play and Lenora "talk" exuberantly to a rag doll. But his smile faded when he realized Ava didn't look happy.

Letting the last note fade, Ava pulled her hands from the keys and frowned at the sheet music in front of her.

"What's wrong, doll?" He got up and walked over to place a hand on her shoulder. "That was beautiful. I've missed your playing."

"It's not the playing, it's the singing."

He couldn't help his smirk. "It wasn't that bad." Though Ava wasn't the singer her sister and mother were, it wasn't as if her voice made dogs whine.

"I can't do the song justice. Mama could have, but now?" Her shoulder shifted under his hand as she shrugged. "It's hard to listen to her sing, knowing how much pain she must be in."

He swallowed and let his hand fall from her shoulder. He'd

27

noticed Leah's gravelly voice, but how had he not realized the accident would've ruined her lovely singing, too—no, *he* had ruined her singing. "Pain? Should she sing at all then?"

The thought alone kicked him in the gut. How many years had he woken up to his wife humming a beautiful tune as she prepared breakfast? Stopped singing in the middle of church just to listen to his wife pour her heart out to the Lord? And he'd taken that away from her by letting his lust for money destroy his family.

"Doctor hasn't said she shouldn't as far as I know, but listening to her, it has to hurt. She wouldn't admit it though. So I thought I'd try to sing, but no one's going to be happy with that—even I can tell I'm flat most the time." She sighed while leaning over to hand Lenora the doll that had fallen out of reach. "This Christmas is not going as I'd hoped. If only Jennie were here."

She turned on the bench to face him. "Can you think of a way to convince Mama not to sing without hurting her feelings? I know she wants to do this for me, but I don't want her to hurt herself."

His throat tightened. "I'm not sure when I'll see your mother next."

"Did she not come with you?" She scrunched her eyebrows and looked past him.

He cleared his throat. "We're, um, not living together. And if she's not coming to dinner…"

Ava blinked up at him. She'd never looked so bewildered, other than that day so many years ago when they'd had to explain how Jennie could no longer see.

He shrugged, dragging his gaze away from hers and down to Lenora, who was chewing on the hem of her doll's dress. "It's what your mother wants."

If anyone deserved to get what she wanted, it was Leah. Though she'd never before asked for something he didn't want to give.

"Hey, you two."

Bryant startled at the low masculine rumble of Oliver's voice behind them.

His son-in-law came over and kissed Ava on the forehead. "Is dinner ready? I'm starving."

At the same time Ava shook her head, Lenora threw her doll and started crying.

Oliver glanced down at his daughter, but walked right past her and out of the room. "I'll bring in more wood then."

Bryant frowned at his son-in-law's retreating back.

Ava huffed and bent to pick up Lenora, shushing her as she bounced her on her knee. "Come now, baby." When the little one didn't stop crying, Ava examined her, but seemed to see nothing of concern. With a few kisses to Lenora's nose and some cooing, the baby finally started to settle.

"That's better." Ava wiped her daughter's puffy eyes and stood, balancing Lenora on her hip. "Can't have you crying while I finish dinner."

"Your mother's not coming to help?"

Ava frowned. "Normally, she'd be here already. I thought she was coming with you."

Bryant reached for Lenora. "Then let me have the baby."

Ava gave him the most unreadable look. Did she not want him to take the baby? But in a flash, she'd handed Lenora over, gave him an exaggerated kiss on his cheek, and left for the kitchen.

Lenora's sniffles changed slightly—sounding less hurt and more worried.

"Not too sure of your Poppop, eh?"

Leaning away, she looked up at him with big, wet eyes.

"Since you know absolutely nothing about me, I bet you'll be the easiest woman in this town to win over." He shoved around her toys with his foot to make an open spot on the rug, then sat down, propping her up in front of him.

Her lower lip began to quiver.

With a silly voice, he squawked. "Oh, no you don't."

Her eyes widened, but her lip stopped quivering.

Leaning over, he picked up the rag doll which had vexed her earlier. Using the same silly voice, he made the toy dance and sing on the rug in front of her. "Mama doesn't want you to cry. Poppop doesn't either."

He wriggled the doll against Lenora's neck to tickle her. "Don't you cry."

She squirmed, a smile threatening her down-turned lips, so he plunged the doll into her roly-poly neck again. "Don't you do it."

She scrunched up to ward off his tickles, but her eyes lit and a two-nubby-toothed grin broke through.

Did anyone else think she looked exactly like her Aunt Jennie?

He kept his smile in place, but the same emptiness he'd struggled against while incarcerated filled him. How he'd missed his girls. But only one was happy to see him.

"Nope, there will be two. I'll win you over." He cupped his granddaughter's chubby cheek. "But you'll forget all about me if I leave, won't you?"

Lenora turned wary again, so he released her and picked up the doll to make it recite "Peas Porridge Hot."

If he had to leave, if this was the last time his family would be together, maybe he should plead for Jennie to come home for Christmas. He'd do anything to give Ava the happy holiday memory she wanted before she learned it could be the family's last.

He'd have to sell his rifle or something to get his youngest home, but he'd pray she'd agree. The last time she'd written, she'd seemed intent on staying in the city.

He'd figured he'd have a good chance at finding work in Chicago, but he'd expected Leah to move with him since it'd be close to one of their daughters. But if she wouldn't, did they have any choice but to separate?

Unable to maintain the silly voice he was using to entertain Lenora, he set the dolly down, scooped his granddaughter up, and squeezed her tight. Thankfully, she didn't protest.

How could he endure being so far away he couldn't check up on these three every day? Seven months of being uncertain of how they fared had been pure torture. If he didn't leave on good terms…

No. Leaving town was not an option. He must find something to do here.

CHAPTER FOUR

The laundry door bell jangled as Corinne Key, the previous laundress, came in, her face beaming. Her blond hair was windswept, her cheeks and nose a rosy pink.

Leah cranked the last sheet through the wringer, then came up to the counter. "What brings you in this icy afternoon? You look happier than anyone should be when it's eighteen degrees outside."

"I am." Corinne plunked her elbows on the counter, rubbing her arms despite them being ensconced in a thick wool coat. She leaned forward. "I really am."

Leah couldn't help but smile back.

Corinne leaned closer. "Because you were right," she whispered.

"About what?" Leah chuckled at her friend's exuberant vagueness.

"Your advice." She lifted her eyebrows and glanced toward the door. "About, you know…things."

"Oh." Leah forced the smile to stay on her face. Corinne's happiness was no reason to feel sad. And yet, would she ever again sport such a silly grin after a night with her own husband? She'd been glad to offer the newlywed bride advice, but it hurt to know she'd not be enjoying Bryant's attentions anytime soon.

Corinne's cheeks turned redder than what winter weather would cause. "I had to duck in here because everyone keeps asking me why I'm smiling so much. And if they guessed, I'd be mortified! But I'm stuck in town until Nolan finishes his errands."

Patting Corinne's hand, Leah's smile felt real again. "I'm surprised he dragged you into town with the weather being what it is."

"Oh, well, he didn't want to, but the men are going to quit on him if he keeps putting off getting supplies to cozy up with me."

The door jangled and the man in question came in along with a waft of glacial wind.

The second Nolan caught sight of his wife, he grinned and walked straight for her. "I'm done at the mercantile. We can go home now."

Leah shook her head. Did he even notice she was standing there?

Corinne turned toward her and whispered, "Thanks so much."

Nolan jolted.

Seemed he hadn't noticed her. She started to chuckle, but Nolan only winked at her before tugging his wife up against his side. "Good day, Mrs. Whitsett."

And with that, they were out the door. Before Leah could shake her head and get back to work, Celia barged in.

"I'm sorry I said I couldn't help you with the holiday rush." She shed her coat and grabbed an apron. "I only said that because I didn't want to, but I've felt guilty all day. So I'll help, whether I want to or not."

"Celia." She stayed the young lady with a hand around her arm. "You don't have to work. I only asked if you wanted some hours."

"You wouldn't have asked unless you needed someone." Celia pulled away.

"True, but—"

"What do you want me to do first?" Celia unbuttoned a shirt cuff, readying to roll up her sleeve.

Leah stopped her. "Honey, you shouldn't feel guilty about what happened to me anymore. If you don't want to help—"

"It's not about that." Celia stepped back, continuing to roll up her sleeve. "Not that I don't still feel guilty about what happened to you because of me—but rather, I feel guilty because I'm not doing anything good with my time." The young woman huffed, grabbed a basket of wet laundry, and headed into the back room.

Another gust of wind brought Ava through the front door.

Goodness, was everyone going to visit today? Leah shivered against the new bout of cold air. "What brings y—"

"Why aren't you living with Papa?"

Leah's palms grew sweaty despite the fact she'd just shivered seconds ago. She ought to tell Ava that was none of her business, but could she truly defend her decision? In a way her daughter would accept?

Ava stopped at the counter and clasped it. "How can you give me advice about my marriage when you're not trying to save your own?"

Save? Did it need saving? Of course it did.

"Mama, wasn't it you who told me at my wedding that no matter how I feel, from one day to the next, I should remind myself that I love my husband and base what I do next on that?"

Leah's shoulders tightened. "Yes, but going to prison for helping your boss swindle people in order to hide a gambling debt is a far piece different than not picking up your socks."

"That's not what you meant that day." Ava leaned forward. "You weren't talking about silly irritations."

"I was including them."

Celia marched back in. "Is there more to hang?"

Before Leah could point to the second basket, Celia found it and headed back to where Corinne had mounted an ingenious tiered clothesline in the backroom for whenever the weather was nasty.

The second Celia was out of the room, Ava leaned even closer. "Papa messed up horrifically, there's no arguing that. But everyone's flawed, Mama. You can't turn your back on your vows because your husband messes up hugely any more than you can if he messes up slightly. It's all part of the 'for better and worse and good times and bad,' right?"

Leah closed her eyes and exhaled slowly. She'd not argue with her daughter. Ava had always been her father's girl.

Though when had her daughter become so sure of everything? Hadn't she just talked Ava out of an exaggerated sense of doom last week?

"Papa needs your forgiveness. Just like me. Just like Celia." Ava gestured toward the back of the laundry. "Look what your forgiveness has done for her. She's become responsible, wanting to live up to what you see in her. Imagine what Papa could become if you forgave him as freely as you have her—and maybe even more so because it'll be hard for you to do."

Opening her eyes, Leah couldn't help releasing a sigh at what her daughter couldn't understand. "Celia didn't hurt me."

"Of course she did." Ava pointed at her mother's eyebrow. "Your scars, the limp. It was more her doing than Papa's."

"She didn't mean to."

"Neither did Papa."

"He was older, wiser—"

"Mama…"

She had to look away to keep from tearing up. Why *was* it a hundred times more difficult to forgive him than anyone else involved in the accident that had caused her scars?

She'd forgiven Celia the moment she'd regained consciousness, so why had she held onto her resentment toward Bryant for more than half a year? Though one thing was certain. She couldn't just force herself to forgive because someone told her to.

Steeling herself, she turned to face her daughter, just as the front door slammed behind Ava.

Cold flooded her body.

What if her relationship with Ava grew strained over this? What if Ava would no longer want her help if Bryant left and she remained behind?

But she couldn't throw herself back into his arms and act as if everything was all right.

She turned back to the linens she'd started soaking. For the next two hours with Celia working beside her, she tried to keep her focus on getting things done, but all she could think about was how avoiding Celia wouldn't have helped either of them. So, though it might feel better to ignore Bryant, she just couldn't continue doing so if she was going to be an adult about this.

An hour before closing, Leah stopped Celia from grabbing another bag of laundry. "Why don't you head home?"

The young lady's eyebrows scrunched as she took a quick glance at the wall clock.

"Actually, it's me who needs to go home." Her voice shook saying that out loud, but thankfully the girl wouldn't know why.

"All right." Celia untied her apron and hung it up. "I'll come in tomorrow after chores."

"I'll see you then."

After Celia left, Leah flipped over the sign and slumped onto the bench near the counter.

God...

She closed her eyes. It'd been so long since she'd prayed. She didn't deserve to be heard, and yet, how did she have any hope to do what Ava wanted—no, what she ought to do, without His help?

The problem is I don't want to do this. I don't feel like it at all.

After a few more minutes, realizing she had no words worth

praying, she headed up to pack what little she had in the laundry's upstairs apartment.

Once she'd finished, she forged out into the cold. Within minutes, she found herself thankful for the freezing temperature despite how it sharpened the pain in her hip, for it forced her forward. The hope of sitting in front of the living room's fireplace was something her legs were willing to limp toward.

At the front door, she opted not to knock and turned the knob.

In the green chair—his chair—Bryant was slumped against the headrest, his shirt open at the collar, his jacket off.

It was hard to swallow. He was still so handsome, and she... wasn't.

His head rolled to the side, and his gaze swept over her, almost as if he wasn't seeing her, then landed at the bags near her feet. He pushed himself up from the chair with a start.

She put out a hand. "Things haven't changed between us. I'm only here because of Ava. I'm taking the guest room."

He took one more hesitant step, then stopped. "Because of Ava?"

"If I ignore her wishes, I could end up losing what I have with her. So I'm here for Christmas."

"Only Christmas?"

She shrugged, as if saying what she would say next was easy. "And afterward."

He stood quite stiff. "I couldn't find a job, and I looked all day."

"Then what are you going to do?"

Though he still stood upright, he appeared to lose an inch or two. "As I said before, I haven't much choice. I'll have to look for work elsewhere, and I want you to come—"

"No." Her head shook of its own accord.

"Leah—"

She picked up her bags and walked past him. "My hip hurts too much to stand here and argue the obvious. I won't leave."

37

"Then how are we going to survive?"

The break in his voice halted her steps, but she didn't turn. His inflection made it clear he wasn't only talking about finances.

Her breathing grew shallow. "How can I trust you'll do better for me elsewhere when you failed me here, when we had everything we needed?" She turned to look at him. "You left me with an empty bank account. You left me alone. I can't blindly follow you again. I've got the laundry. That'll be enough."

"But the banker said—"

"He's just waiting for you to tell him you have no objections to me running the laundry. He'll write up a contract as soon as you do."

"And if I'm not fine with that?"

She narrowed her eyes. "Don't you leave me unable to provide for myself."

Returning home to him wasn't going at all like Ava had likely hoped.

"That's just it, Leah." Bryant took a step forward, his hands out in front of him as if begging for a hot meal. "I want to provide for you."

"But you didn't." The bitterness in her voice made her inhale sharply—yet, what she'd said was the truth.

He lowered his hands to his sides, his mossy green eyes dulling. "What if the laundry isn't enough?" His voice had dropped to just above a whisper. "I heard Corinne had to give it up because she couldn't keep up with it. What if that happens to you? With your injuries—"

"There's no guarantee you can sustain me either. We were doing fine before last year. We had plenty of money. We were comfortable. We had a grandchild on the way, and yet, you gambled it all away. You chose greed over our family's good name."

"You're right, I did. And then I tried to cover it up with one mistake after another. But I didn't go along with McGill just for my own welfare. I did it because I so desperately didn't want to fail you. Or rather, to admit just how badly I had."

"Which means you must realize how difficult it is for me to believe you can fix this now. Surely you have to understand how I feel."

"I don't blame you for how you feel at all." His posture sunk another inch. "If Oliver did to Ava what I did to you, I'd be hard-pressed not to thrash him. I'd only be able to keep from doing so for Ava and Lenora's sake."

"Good, then you can see why we can't leave." Her voice choked. "For Ava and Lenora's sake."

Turning, she scurried toward the guest room before she broke down in tears or he attempted to fold her up in his arms.

The thought of his embrace shot a cold, hard zing through her heart. However, a zing mattered little when her heart had been shattered into so many pieces it might never be put back together.

CHAPTER FIVE

"As much as I wish I could, Bryant, it wouldn't look good to hire someone connected to the mess you were involved in."

"It's just cutting meat, Martin." Bryant forced himself not to lean across the butcher's counter and shake him a little. "You don't have to have me up front. I can stay in the back."

Martin shrugged and let out a shaky breath. "I don't think it'd be good for business."

"What about cleaning up after hours?"

"Jack Boatman does that, and his mother depends on the money."

Bryant made himself breathe before replying. "I understand. If you change your mind, let me know."

"I will."

Bryant turned and walked out as nonchalantly as he could. He wouldn't beg…yet.

Nolan and Jacob had projects he could help with, but neither man had enough money to pay him. Nolan had offered him and Leah a room if things got bad. He hadn't bothered to tell his friend the bunkhouse would suffice since he'd be alone.

Slogging through the slush on the boardwalk, he kept from

looking toward the laundry. He hadn't found employment, and that's all Leah would be interested in.

He scanned the street lined with stores decorated with frosty windowpanes and evergreen wreaths. Was there a shop owner left in this town who hadn't turned him down flat yet? If his wife didn't trust him, how could he expect anyone else to?

Across the way, Harold Seitz, the father of one of Ava's friends, left the mercantile.

Bryant raised a hand in greeting, but Harold quickly looked to his feet as he walked down the road. Bryant tilted his head toward the sky. As hard as it was having friends refuse him employment, being ignored was worse.

Especially by his wife. Last night, he'd had a hard time sleeping after Leah had turned her back on him—the very woman who used to insist they stay up into the wee hours to be sure neither of them went to bed angry.

And last night, she'd gone to bed angry.

He blew out a breath and started walking again. Thankfully he'd had no idea how badly he'd hurt Leah when he'd been carted off to prison. Otherwise, he might have done exactly what Jacob had been afraid he'd do. When his friend had left him this past spring, he'd paid the jailer extra to keep watch on him.

Before last year, he'd have said he'd never kill himself, but after a few months behind bars, his friend had been right—the shame had nearly overwhelmed him. The only thing that had kept him from such a desperate act was his wife. She needed him. She was waiting for him.

The sudden rush of warmth behind his eyes forced himself to hold his breath to keep tears from falling in public.

God loved him. Ava loved him. He had Lenora. But Leah… he'd never thought her love would grow cold. He had to face the fact that she'd finally realized he wasn't the perfect man she used to tell everyone he was.

He clenched his fists and moved down the street, scanning

each window for a help wanted sign. Maybe he could find employment with someone who had no idea who he was. Who didn't know him? Everyone was a friend, an acquaintance, a former coworker...a milliner.

Since when did Armelle have a millinery?

Across the way, a window was filled with women's hats of every color, shape, and size. If he got employed making ladies hats, he'd be the butt of every joke from now until the end of his life. But maybe something needed cleaned or repaired. Bracing himself, he strode over.

The woman behind the counter had ruddy cheeks and dark hair laced with silver—he'd never seen her before.

He released a long exhale.

The lady turned, and her eyes lit. "I bet by the look of you, you've got yourself a gorgeous lady at home in need of a pretty bonnet. Is it her birthday? Anniversary?"

"I'm afraid that's not why I'm here." He tugged on his tie. "I'm looking for work."

"Oh, are you a hatter? Do you work with fur? I could definitely add a men's line—"

"Uh..." The way her eyes kept lighting up made it hard not to give her what she wanted. "I was hoping maybe you needed someone to clean or repair things. I could tie bows if that's all you had for me to do though."

She chuckled. "That'd not take you but a few hours. But if you're desperate enough to do women's work, why not check at the laundry? The other day, I was talking to the owner, a Mrs. Whitsett, about how her new contract with the railroad was going to swamp her."

The milliner might as well have punched him in the gut. Leah needed help? And she didn't tell him?

If he called no more attention to himself, maybe this woman wouldn't recognize him the next time she saw him. "Thank you, ma'am." He tipped his hat and left the shop.

After waiting for a wagon to roll by on the slushy road,

Bryant crossed over to the laundry. He might receive a chilly reception, but it couldn't be any frostier than it was outside.

The door's bell announced his presence, and his wife came in from the back with a stilted smile. Was that because her scarring kept her smile from looking natural, or had she sensed it'd be him standing here?

No need to beat about the bush. "I've asked everybody. And as I thought, no one will hire me."

She stayed where she was. "Maybe you should consider doing something you'd rather not? Laundry's not my favorite thing to do, but that's what's available."

He nodded and took off his jacket. "You're right, that's what's available." He rolled up his sleeves, moved to the closest tub filled with wet clothing, and pulled out a shirt.

"What are you doing?"

"I don't know. Is this ready to scrub or wring?"

She folded her arms. "You expect to do laundry for me?"

"I need work."

"I can't hire you."

He swallowed against the hurt, and kept his gaze fixed on the wet shirt in his hands. "You don't have to pay me." Somehow his voice had come out rougher than hers.

"So you're not leaving town?"

Was there a touch of hope in that question? Though he would do almost anything to bolster any positive emotion toward him, he had to shake his head. "I need to make money at some point. After Christmas—"

"What about Ava and the baby?"

He chanced a look at her, despite knowing her eyes were likely shooting daggers. "Just like Jennie, we can come back and visit on occasion."

"You mean *you* can visit on occasion."

He held his tongue and turned back to the washtub. He couldn't dwell on their impasse—or the possibility that he'd ruined their marriage beyond repair. He held up the shirt. "Scrub?"

When she didn't so much as nod or shake her head, he looked around for a washboard. She likely thought he had no idea what to do, but he'd worked in the prison laundry every week. He set the board in the water against the tub and examined the shirt, noting the dirt on the sleeve. He rubbed the cloth against the corrugated metal, waiting for Leah to tell him he was doing it wrong.

But after a few minutes, she walked off, grabbed a washing dolly, then began agitating a washtub full of clothes with it.

Minutes ticked by in silence, then an hour. After emptying the washtub, he ran a hand through his hair. She still kept her back toward him. Would she not give him any instruction? They used to work so well together. One of his happiest memories was the week they'd repainted their house, talking and laughing the entire time, groaning each night as they dropped into bed, cuddling up despite their protesting muscles.

He let out a loud, impatient breath. "What would you like me to do next?"

She shrugged and continued ironing.

After a few minutes, he swallowed hard, but scanned the room, hoping to figure out something else to do. He wasn't going to force her into a heated conversation when a customer could interrupt at any moment. He headed for the large bags slumped against the wall.

"You can't leave."

He stopped.

Her words had been quiet, heartbreakingly so—but at least she'd said it loud enough for him to hear.

He turned. "Why not? You don't want my help. You don't need me."

"I do need you."

"But you don't. You've proven you can get on fine without me, so much so you're even shunning me."

Silence, yet again.

Except was that a sniffle?

Despite his entire being wanting to rush over and scoop her up, he clamped his arms hard against his sides. He was barely holding onto his self-worth as it was. If she rejected him, how could he remain in her presence?

She sniffled twice more, but kept ironing.

He took a step closer. "My leaving won't be because I want to abandon you. I know I left you in a financial lurch last spring, but I have to go elsewhere if I have any hope of rectifying that. However, if you don't come with me, I trust you can take care of yourself and Ava without me."

"But that's just it." She dropped her wet laundry and whirled on him. "You *didn't* trust me."

He blinked. "Well, I do now. You've proven you can take care of yourself."

"I'm not talking about surviving. What you didn't trust me with was what you were going through. You didn't trust me to be able to help you. You didn't trust me with your secrets, your difficulties, nothing."

He let his shoulders slump. So many times over the past year he'd played out scenarios where he'd told her about every dark thing, every insecurity, every failure. In all those made-up conversations, he'd failed to imagine how exposing his every flaw wouldn't have pushed her away. But could any of those imagined reactions be worse than how things were going now?

"You're right, I didn't trust you." Despite how hushed his voice came out, the words still tore him up. "Though not in the way you think. I could've told you about the gambling. I knew you would've been able to handle it. You would've set me back on the straight and narrow, absolutely. But what I didn't trust you to do was to still love me." He thumped his chest. "*Me.*"

He stared off at nothing, letting his vision fuzz, leaving his fist pressed against his sluggishly beating heart. "You've always loved what you saw in me. You've always looked past my flaws as if they weren't there, seeing the man I could become. However, if I'd laid out my flaws in a way you couldn't have missed, where you'd have realized I was never going to become the hero you believed me to be, I was afraid you'd..." His throat closed up too much to go on.

She didn't say anything, so he finally forced himself to continue. "I love that you wanted to be my encourager—every man wants that—so I tried to live up to your expectations. However, when I ruined everything, I was sure you'd—"

"You thought me capable of hating you?" She stared at him as if he'd taken leave of his senses. "Of leaving you?"

"I didn't expect you to hate me or leave me, no. I was afraid if I didn't become the hero you were so certain I could be, your love for me would never be the same. And I wasn't sure my heart could survive that, or rather, I was sure it couldn't, because *I* hated myself. Why would you be any different?"

She began to walk toward him, and his heavy heartbeat consumed his body.

"Do you love *me* at all anymore?" He scrunched his eyes tight and grimaced. He shouldn't have asked that.

The coolness of her hand cupped his cheek, and when he opened his eyes, he was confronted with the scar that ran through her brow, the droop that weighed down her mouth, the sadness permeating her expression—all the results of his selfishness. "Forgive me?" His question was nothing but a voiceless rush of air and he tensed in anticipation of her answer.

Her hand slipped from his face, and for a moment that seemed like a century, she blinked up at him. No malice shone in her eyes, but then, she wasn't looking at him in that tender way she always did—or rather, used to.

And then she looked down and away. "I...um. It's time to close up the laundry."

Close up?

Yes, that's what he needed to do right now. Close up. Close down. Whatever it took to shut off these emotions.

Leah turned and walked away, picking up wet laundry as she headed to the back room and disappeared.

She hadn't said she loved him. She hadn't forgiven him.

Imagining Leah refusing to forgive anyone was something he'd never thought he'd be able to do.

Which meant...

Jangle, Jangle.

He jolted at the door's opening. "We're closed." His voice rang out harsher and sharper than he'd meant.

When heavy footfalls thudded in anyway, he pushed off the counter and forged through the back room, past his wife, and out into the frigid air.

He couldn't disappoint his wife anymore today. But would he have any better of a chance at winning her over tomorrow? What if his best would never again be enough?

CHAPTER SIX

Down on her knees, Leah scrubbed the kitchen's baseboard a second time. Her hip throbbed, her joints screamed, yet she continued. She wouldn't get up until everything was spotless—and Bryant was sure to be asleep.

She glanced toward the hallway, where her husband had stood not more than an hour ago. When she'd told him she didn't need his help cleaning the kitchen, he'd stood there for a long time. Sadness had radiated off him so thickly, she'd nearly crumpled.

But she'd kept scrubbing.

Today, they'd worked in silence at the laundry for the second day in a row. She'd not allowed herself to speak, even on their walk home. For what was there to say?

He'd already asked her to forgive him, if she still loved him. And she'd said nothing.

She'd wanted to tell him she'd forgiven him, but she wasn't certain she had. He'd looked so crushed that to give him some hope, she'd crossed the room to cup his face.

And then all her words had jammed up.

Touching him, well…

She shook her head and dunked her cloth in the bucket

again. Touching him had stirred up such a slurry of emotions that half of her had wanted to kick him in the shins, and the other half had wanted to step into his arms and weep.

Leah wrung dirty water out of her rag and started scouring again.

Before she'd gotten herself sorted out, Bryant had left and Celia had come in with a load of laundry. The young lady hadn't seemed to notice anything wrong. In fact, she'd worn a grin through most of their discussion. How long had it been since that girl had smiled? Not only was Celia smiling now, but whenever she helped in the laundry, there was no awkwardness between them—despite how the girl had been partially responsible for every scar Leah had.

But with Bryant, even mornings were awkward. Since she'd returned to the house last week, she never could decide if she wanted to ask him what he wanted for breakfast or force him to fend for himself.

She slapped the rag back into the bucket of water, sloshing the foamy slush onto the floorboards.

She *had* to forgive him, but how to do so when her emotions were completely opposed? She'd expected them to mellow with time, but waiting for her feelings to change toward Bryant wasn't doing either of them any good.

After shoving the bucket and rag under the sink, she crossed to the kitchen table and snatched up her Bible. She normally read a passage or two while drinking coffee in the morning, but waiting until then wouldn't do them any good now, either.

She blew out the lanterns and trudged upstairs. What should she read? Were there any marriage reconciliation stories that could help? Hosea and his wife, maybe? No, Bryant hadn't cheated on her, nor continued to do so—but he had betrayed her trust. Hosea's story did illustrate that God loved the disloyal Israelites no matter what they did. She certainly ought to do that in regard to her own husband, but how could she make herself want to?

Maybe Ruth and Boaz's story would be better.

In the guest room, she dressed for the night, then turned the flame down, curling up on the bed with her Bible, determined to read the whole story, hoping to glean something.

Half an hour later, she closed the book, rolled onto her back, and stared at the ceiling.

Had Ruth felt love toward Boaz when she'd lain at his feet? Maybe she had, maybe she hadn't. The story simply recorded that Ruth did as her mother-in-law instructed, believing all things would be well because of the God Naomi served, for whom Ruth had given up everything to follow.

And because of that trust, Ruth had acted, and her obedience resulted in a fruitful union. *Acting* in faith—was that the key?

Pushing herself up to sit on the edge of the mattress, Leah put on her slippers, smoothed her nightdress, and blew out the light.

Then stood and put one foot in front of the other.

Not worried about waking Bryant since he was a heavy sleeper, she crossed the hallway and opened the door to their room.

In the dark, she listened to his soft breathing and contemplated the foot of the bed. No, sleeping there would be strange. Her side of the bed would do.

Leah picked her way across the room and slipped under the covers. The second his warmth registered, every bit of tension rushed out of her, the familiarity nearly making her cry. After seven months alone, the comforting smell she could only describe as belonging to her husband made her body relax more than it had since the night she'd almost been killed. The pull to snuggle into him was so overwhelming, she had to flip over.

She blinked unseeingly into the blackness for a while. Turning her back on him was not the point of this exercise. Pulling in a fortifying breath, she rolled back over and gently placed a hand on him. A symbol of sorts, indicating her dependence on him, like Ruth with Boaz.

She might have told Bryant she didn't need him, but she was only kidding herself. If he could feel she intended to stay by his side, maybe he wouldn't leave. With Oliver and Ava's struggles, with Lenora just learning who he was, they needed him here.

Bryant's soft breathing continued unaltered. Within minutes, the rhythmic rise and fall of his chest, the smell of his bedclothes, the warmth of his body pulled her closer. Her nights of tossing and turning without him beside her were over.

If only her heart would figure things out soon.

Something stirred. Bryant opened his eyes to complete darkness. It was far too early to be awake. He forced himself to lie still and listen. What had awoken him?

And then a soft breath registered against his neck, causing him to shiver. Leah.

He froze. Had she gotten up in the middle of the night and walked in half asleep out of habit? Slowly, he rolled toward her. The silkiness of her hair cascading off his arm made him clench his hands to keep from scooping her up and threading his fingers into her long, soft tresses.

Should he wake her? Let her know she'd accidentally wandered in after a trip to the necessary?

Crossing his arms over his chest, he stared up at the ceiling he couldn't see. It'd be best to go back to sleep. To let her awake before he did, so she'd not know that he knew she'd ended up where she hadn't wanted to be. Oh, how that hurt.

How many times over the years had Leah said she couldn't stand the thought of them being apart and begged that he wouldn't die before she did?

But now, the only reason she was under the same roof was because of Ava's wishes.

Unable to help himself, he turned to take in her silhouette as the subtle gray of morning crept in. He took up one soft curl and rubbed it between his fingers.

Having her choose to *endure* him rather than *live* with him was worse than anything he'd ever imagined back in prison.

Jacob had warned Bryant not to give in to dark thoughts. His friend had encouraged him to serve his time, get out, and live again. But the dark thoughts had come anyway. At one point, he'd stopped talking to the other inmates, even gave up eating, but Jacob had insisted on leaving behind a Bible, and the uncanny pull of a God who wouldn't let go had tugged at him.

Reading over the many stories demonstrating how God never stopped loving His wayward children, a bubble of hope had emerged—that no matter what he'd done, God wouldn't leave him—and that his wife, a woman of such grace, wouldn't leave him either. He'd begun eating again, forcing himself through the motions of living, so he could return home and set things right.

Though once he'd returned to Armelle, the darkness had threatened to drag him back down. He'd always said he didn't deserve Leah—and now, he knew that with certainty. His actions had turned his compassionate wife into a woman who could actually hold a grudge—

Her head rolled toward him, and he stiffened.

Please don't wake up.

Her eyelids fluttered, and he held his breath. After a blink or two, she looked straight at him for one second, then another.

He braced himself for her to stiffen once she realized she'd somehow ended up beside him.

She kept looking at him, her lashes fluttering on occasion as her eyes cleared of sleep.

"I'm sorry," he whispered. "I didn't mean to wake you. I know you didn't mean to come in here—"

"I did."

What? "On purpose?"

Her head made a slight dip. "I just... I..." Her eyes closed, and she nestled her head back into her pillow. Maybe she hadn't actually awakened.

"It's not that I can't," she whispered, followed by several soft, even breaths. "It's just that I don't want to." She yawned. "Which isn't right, so I thought I could."

He clamped his mouth so he wouldn't ask her to explain. Her incoherent babble indicated she was still asleep. When they'd first married, her sleep talking had awakened him several times. Perhaps she'd never stopped talking in her sleep and he'd learned to sleep through it.

"I thought I'd trick my body into liking you again, but I mif... I can't. I wanna but..." And with another slur of unintelligible syllables, her breathing slowed, and her body went slack.

She was trying to trick herself into liking him?

What if she woke up in the morning and felt as if her "trick" hadn't worked and she never returned to his side again?

Though he'd be worse off if such a nightmare came true, he wedged his hand under her and pulled her as close as he dared so as not to wake her. Turning his face into his pillow, he muffled the sound of his heart being rent in two.

How low could a man sink before all hope disintegrated?

CHAPTER SEVEN

The back door to the church banged open, causing Leah to drop the greenery she was winding around the railing.

A bark echoed through the sanctuary, then another.

"Is there a dog inside the church?" Leah turned to her daughter, who was decorating the piano.

Before Ava could answer, the Keys' black dog ran into the sanctuary, wearing a chemise with … cotton stuck to it? "What in the world?"

Spencer ran in after the canine, sporting a huge smile. "Mickey's going to be our sheep!"

"Our sheep?" She took in the dog's costume, which twisted around his torso with his every bouncy step.

"See, I told you no one would know what he was." Celia followed them in, her scowl firmly in place. "He looks ridiculous."

"So did that pig you dressed up in Mrs.—"

"Shhh." Leah widened her eyes at the boy and scanned the sanctuary, hoping Mrs. Tate hadn't slipped back in with the candles. The recollection of that pig wearing the older woman's undergarments never failed to bring a smile to her face—especially since it shouldn't.

Spencer crossed his arms and narrowed his eyes at his sister. "Doesn't matter what you say anyway. Mrs. Key said I could dress Mickey up if I wanted to. Said everyone should 'fodder a kid's creativity'."

Celia punched him in the shoulder. "*Foster.*"

He ducked despite having already been hit. "That's what I said!"

"Mrs. Key doesn't get to make the decision, anyway. Mrs. Ronstandt does." Celia pointed toward the dog as if he were on trial for something heinous. "And she's not going to allow a dog in cotton-covered undergarments to be a sheep. If she wants a sheep, there's plenty of sheep around Armelle."

He flung his arms open wide. "Nothing's real in this pageant. Jesus is a girl, and *you're* a boy—"

"And you're certainly no angel."

He planted his hands on his hips and nodded as if that settled the matter. "So the dog can be a sheep."

"*If* Mrs. Ronstandt says so." Celia lifted her brows as she looked to Ava, her eyes wide and pleading.

Ava shrugged. "I don't mind."

"Yay!" Spencer grabbed the dog's paws and danced with him while Celia groaned.

A clatter sounded at the back of the church, and Leah cringed. She looked over to where Lenora had been laid on a pallet of blankets—still asleep thankfully.

"Can someone help, please?" Jacob's voice called out.

Minutes later, he and Ava dragged in a ladder and a long coil of rope.

"You're really going to fly him?" Leah couldn't stop her chuckle.

Jacob's grin was cheeky. "Always wanted to fly when I was a kid."

Though her daughter's childhood dream wasn't going as she'd hoped, Leah was proud that Ava was willing to make this a wonderful memory for Spencer. "He'll remember this forever

—though you may regret it. He'll want you to fly him every year."

Jacob dropped the ladder near the back wall. "I saw Bryant's arms the other day. He can take over for me next year."

She refused to let her smile slip, so she busied herself with the greenery again. How long until everyone knew Bryant intended to leave her? Would he even be back next Christmas?

The foyer doors banged open behind her, letting in a rush of cold air.

"Merry Christmas, everybody." Bryant's voice was followed immediately by Ava's squeal, and then their daughter abandoned the candles she'd been arranging to run off the platform.

Why would she react like that?

"Merry Christmas," a softer, feminine voice called.

Leah's heart stopped. Could it be? She turned, unable to breathe.

Ava ran straight down the aisle, nearly knocking over her younger sister as they crashed into an embrace.

"Jennie," Leah breathed. She picked her way around the boxes of decorations to get to her youngest, who looked even more like a woman than the last time she'd seen her.

Within seconds, she'd wrapped herself into a giant hug between her two girls. After holding them tight for a few moments, she peeked over at Bryant through blurry eyes. He hadn't moved from the doorway, his stance both hopeful and sad, like a puppy being denied the chance to play.

She waved him over, and in seconds, he'd pulled them into his arms, crushingly hard.

Ava backed away first and swept Jennie's dark hair off her forehead, slipping right back into her role as sibling protector. "I can't believe you're here."

Jennie's smile wavered. "It's been a while."

Leah pulled her youngest to her, reveling in the feel of her girl being back in her arms.

"Where's Oliver and the baby?" Bryant's gruff voice drew

Leah's attention off Jennie. "Weren't you all practicing for the nativity?"

Though Ava's countenance didn't change, her sparkle disappeared. "Oliver's not going to be in it."

"What do you mean?"

"Celia's playing Joseph!" Spencer waved a shepherd's staff from up at the front of the church.

Bryant looked to Ava, then to Celia, who'd put on her costume. "But you're a—"

"Doesn't matter." Celia shrugged and slipped the covering up over her head. "No one will know."

Leah let go of Jennie and took a step closer to her husband, keeping her voice low. "Oliver isn't interested in playacting. And with him ignoring Lenora, and not—"

Bryant clasped her arm. "What?"

She frowned at the slight jerk, but the scowl on his face wasn't aimed at her. She lowered her voice despite Ava having already moved away. "We think Oliver's unhappy about the baby being a girl, but he'll get over it. Though not quick enough to take part in this."

"Why didn't Ava tell me?"

"She likely expected Mama to." Jennie's voice tore Leah's gaze from her husband's. Though she'd lost her vision years ago after falling out of a hayloft, Jennie had never lost the ability to read her sister.

Jennie took hold of Leah's arm. Her daughter's eyebrows, so like her own, rose above her glossy green eyes. A silent accusation hung in the air between them.

She couldn't begin to explain to Jennie why she'd hardly spoken to Bryant, much less why she hadn't told him about Oliver.

"Are you all right, Mama?"

She stiffened.

"If you want to sing instead of me, I don't want to take that from you. But Papa seemed to think—"

"Oh, of course." Jennie had thought she was upset about no longer singing. "I don't have to sing the song. I'll be glad to accompany."

Spencer ran up to them. "You want me to help you onto the stage, Miss Whitsett?"

Jennie reached out and bumped into his chest. Her face lit as she moved her hand up to ruffle his hair. "My, how you've grown."

"But not too much." He ducked away from getting ruffled further. "Otherwise, they'd not let me fly."

"I heard about that on the way over."

Continuing to babble about one thing after another, Spencer escorted Jennie down the aisle toward the front. Once Jennie made it up the stairs, Ava's face lit at something her sister must have said, and the two promptly moved to the piano bench. Ava opened the music, a genuine smile adorning her lips.

"Thank you for getting Jennie here." Leah's heart warmed at the sight of their daughters' heads bent together. "I believe you've made Ava quite happy."

"But are you happy?"

Something in his tone made her wary. "Of course I am. Ever since I found out Oliver wouldn't participate, I've wished Jennie could come, but—"

"If you wanted her here, why didn't you ask me to get her?"

Why did he sound hurt? "I didn't want to take Jennie away from the life she's making for herself in Chicago."

"I understand that, but why aren't you asking me for anything?"

She frowned up at him. "What are you talking about?"

"Why didn't you tell me what's going on with Oliver?"

She squirmed. "It's been going on for so long. I didn't think—"

"What's going on exactly?"

She shrugged. "He's like a lot of other men. Says the house-work and the baby aren't his responsibility. So Ava's been upset and overwhelmed. I've been trying to help her as much as I can, but that doesn't make up for how she feels."

"Why was I not told about this?" Bryant ran a hand through his hair. "I failed you terribly—I know that can't be disregarded. But have I ever ignored our girls? Do my failures make me completely unworthy of being involved in their lives?"

"I didn't say that." She caught herself from putting a hand on his arm.

"But you're acting like it." He pointed toward the front of the church where Celia was slumped on the step in her Joseph costume, absently petting the dog's matted cotton clumps. "Have you forgotten the Christmas story? I know you aren't Jesus, but if you can't—" He sighed and shook his head, looking away.

A shiver swept through her and she hugged herself. She definitely wasn't Jesus. In fact, she felt as far away from God as she'd ever been.

Bryant massaged his brow, his fingers spanning the width of his forehead. "Even if you can't forgive me, please don't keep me in the dark about my girls. Please."

"Bryant, I—"

But he turned and walked right out the church's front doors.

The frigid wind that blew in past him made her hug herself harder, just as she had this morning when she'd awoken in their bed—alone. He'd cuddled up to her at some point in the night, but he'd not been there when morning had spilled in its light. Had he gotten up early to meet Jennie's train? Or maybe he'd not wanted to stay beside her, considering the way she'd treated him since his return. Maybe he hadn't meant to cuddle up to her at all.

Turning, she stared blankly at Spencer running across the platform, Jacob atop the ladder, calling for his boy to settle down, and the stained glass window behind the pulpit, depicting Jesus in the Garden. The red shards of glass splayed across Christ's forehead glowed in the pale afternoon light.

Out of love, God had laid down His life for all men—despite their immense failures.

Oh God, I don't feel that kind of love.

Yet, Jesus hadn't felt like dying that day either. However, He'd sacrificed himself for their good despite that—and in doing so, provided many with the grace they didn't deserve and a joy they could share with Him forever.

How could she do less for one of her loved ones when God had given up His glory to come down and do so much for her?

The rhythmic sound of ax splitting wood led Bryant to the back of Ava's house. He rubbed his arms briskly against the snow in the air. If he'd known Oliver would be outside, he'd have swung by the house and grabbed his warmer coat.

Around the corner, he caught sight of his burly son-in-law in a hat pulled low over his brow, the air around him heavy with the white puffs of his labored breathing.

He nodded when his son-in-law caught sight of him, then stood to the side with his arms crossed, waiting for Oliver to finish splitting the log.

When Oliver set down his ax, Bryant stepped closer. "Why aren't you at the church? They're going over the Christmas program now."

His son-in-law leaned heavily on his ax and reached up to brush the perspiration from his face. "I'm not needed for that."

"Yes, you are."

Oliver didn't look at him, just took out a handkerchief and dabbed at his neck. "The Hendrix kids wanted to be in it. Celia's playing Joseph's part."

"Only because of you."

Oliver eyed him.

Bryant moved toward the younger man. His past mistakes wouldn't keep him from trying to stop his girls' husbands from making their own. "Ever since our church started this nativity thing, Ava's been looking forward to having a family and getting to be in it, and yet I've heard you've refused."

Oliver looked away. "I'm not comfortable being up front."

"Playing Joseph? If Celia can muster up the courage to hide behind that head cloth thing, so can you."

Oliver shook his head. "I don't think you have the right to lecture me—"

"My failures are a very good reason for listening to me." Bryant stabbed the air with his finger. "But this isn't about that. This comes down to you being selfish."

"*You're* reprimanding *me* for being selfish?"

Bryant stepped closer. "Judge me for protecting my pride all you want. But how's it going to hurt you to fulfill Ava's wishes? More importantly, what will you gain if you do? I promise you, it'll be more than the pride you could lose. And if anyone looks down on you for making your wife's Christmas wish come true —by portraying the true meaning of Christmas—then they aren't worth impressing."

Oliver's face was hard, but he let his ax handle fall to the ground beside him. "Fine. I'll ask her if she still wants me to do it."

Bryant leaned down to toss Oliver's last split log onto the pile. "I guarantee you she will—as long as she believes you've changed your mind out of love for her."

Oliver huffed, but stuffed his hands into his pockets, and without another word, marched past Bryant and headed for the street.

Following, Bryant lengthened his stride to catch up with his taller son-in-law. Though Oliver had started in the right direction, he needed to be reminded of what was even more important. "You know, I wouldn't have let you marry Ava if I hadn't believed you when you told me she was the best thing that ever happened to you."

Oliver scuffled along, not looking at him. "She is."

"And part of the reason she is, is because of how I treated her as a child." If only he'd been here when the baby had been born to help Oliver see how much he was needed from the beginning. "I've heard you're not spending much time with Lenora."

Though Oliver kept trudging through the snow covering the boardwalks, he'd stiffened. Since he hadn't offered up an excuse, he likely knew he had none.

Bryant followed him past several closed shops, their windows decorated with pine boughs and red ribbon. "I worked hard to make sure my girls felt loved every day, even when they were too small to do much but blink at me. And because of that, I believe they've got a lot of love to give. Withholding affection from Lenora will only make you at fault if your future son-in-law doesn't think she's the best thing that ever happened to him. And if he does think so—well, it'll be in spite of you."

Oliver glared back over his shoulder. "I've heard you say Leah was the best thing that ever happened to you. So why do *you* think you can give me advice? I don't need it."

And yet the young man still marched toward the church.

What Oliver said couldn't be denied. He'd hurt Leah more than he ever thought possible. "Maybe you don't need my words, but you can learn from my mistakes."

"It's only a Christmas program."

"Right." Bryant tried not to glare a hole into the back of his son-in-law's head. "Something easy. Be grateful you've got the chance to fix things before you've piled one sin atop another and ruined everything."

Oliver didn't slow. "Working isn't a sin. I have to work. And then I'm tired—"

"You're so tired you choose to chop firewood over playing with a baby?"

Oliver kept marching.

Bryant moved to catch up. "Right now, she's too young to realize there's been any neglect on your part, and it won't take you as long to get back into your wife's good graces as it'll take me, that's for certain."

Snow crunching under their boots was all that sounded for a bit.

Oliver sighed. "I don't know what to do with a girl."

"Then ask. God wouldn't give you a girl if He knew you couldn't be a good father to her. Besides, if you're holding out on Lenora hoping for a son to come along, you might end up with an estranged daughter and a distant wife."

Oliver took a step onto the church porch but stopped.

Bryant moved around him and pulled open the door. "Celia agreed to be Joseph because she can hide behind the costume, but I'd encourage you to embrace the role of Saint Joseph. He was a man who surrendered what he'd hoped for to do what was best for those he loved. No one looks down on a man like that."

Oliver nodded and walked through the door.

Bryant followed, but stopped on the foyer's rug. How could he follow Joseph's example himself when Leah wanted nothing from him?

God, how can I do what's best for my wife without a job? Is that not what I'm supposed to be striving for? Please show me what to do, and I'll do it—even if it breaks my heart.

Since his past actions had broken Leah's—it would be a fair trade.

CHAPTER EIGHT

Leah handed another soapy dish to Jennie, trying not to glance through the kitchen doorway to the front room. But she failed. Again. Bryant was flat on his stomach in the middle of the rug, mirroring every one of Lenora's exaggerated movements and comical grunts.

Earlier, their granddaughter had loudly voiced her frustration over being stuck on her belly, unable to retrieve the spoon she loved to toss. So Bryant had flopped down beside her and caterwauled along with her, snapping her out of her tirade. Now she was giggling at everything he mimicked, flailing on purpose to keep up his shenanigans.

But Bryant's heart-melting love for his granddaughter wasn't the only reason Leah couldn't stop looking toward the front room. Several minutes ago, Oliver had joined them—on the floor.

He wasn't doing anything silly, but he'd picked up the spoon and had tapped it on the floor, encouraging his daughter to keep trying for it. He was actually playing with her—pathetically in comparison to Bryant—but it was certainly more than he'd ever done before, at least in front of her. In fact, had she ever heard him speak to Lenora?

Bryant must have talked Oliver into playing.

She'd never had to ask Bryant to love on their girls—he just did. He'd always been so present, so available, even after many a long day at the office. She'd taken his love for them all for granted.

Tears formed, but since her hands were covered in greasy water, she had to use her sleeve to wipe them away.

"Mama?"

"Oh." She handed Jennie the next dish. How long had her daughter been standing there with nothing to do? The backdoor opened as Ava returned from the root cellar.

"Ava said she'd like me to stay the night. She finished my book in one sitting. Can you believe it? She wants to talk with me about it."

Ava stomped the snow from her boots. "Did you have a chance to read it, Mama?"

"I'm afraid I haven't." After rehearsal last night, Jennie had told them she'd written a miniature biography of sorts, a collection of stories illustrating what her blindness had taught her about the world. She'd handed each one of her family a bundle of papers to be certain they were all right with how she'd portrayed the family. "I did start it, but I fell asleep."

Ava made a tsking noise, imitating the sound Leah used to make when the girls were young and tactless. "Jennie's going to think you thought her book boring."

"I don't, I—" Well, the truth wasn't anything she wanted to share. She'd worked late at the laundry again for the sole purpose of avoiding their father. And the girls would chastise her for it. And they'd be right to do so.

"It's not boring, Jennie," Ava said in a more serious tone. "It's really good."

"Right." Leah turned to her youngest. "It wasn't your book, honey. I was just exhausted."

"Then make sure you turn in early tonight so you can read it. I think you'll love it." Ava crossed to the kitchen doorway.

"Oliver? Would you get the guest room ready for Jennie? She's agreed to stay over."

"I suppose I could, if…" Oliver hauled himself off the floor, ambled over, then flicked the mistletoe hanging from the doorway. "If I get paid in advance."

Ava looked up. "Where did that come from?"

"Your father put it up. He's trying to help me get back into your good graces."

She bumped his shoulder with her own. "You weren't anywhere close to having to sleep outside—yet."

With a smile on her face, Leah turned away as Oliver leaned down for a kiss.

"There are days I wish I was more than blind," Jennie grumbled loudly. "I can hear your lips smacking from all the way over here."

"Ewww, stop it, Mama and Papa. My eyes, my eyes!" Bryant's high-pitched little girl voice caused Ava to chuckle and break the kiss.

"Oh, thank goodness," Bryant said. He'd been holding the baby's chubby little fists over her eyes. "I think it's safe to look now, Lenora."

When he pulled her arms down, she giggled then started bouncing, clearly anticipating a game of peek-a-boo.

The lack of tension in this house was so welcome after these past few weeks. Perhaps something about Jennie being home made them all relax.

Ava walked into the living room and took the baby from Bryant. "That was nothing, Lenora. Not compared to what Grandma and Poppop used to put me and Aunt Jennie through."

Leah's smile faded. Were all of her warm, romantic memories things of the past?

Oliver passed behind them on his way to the guest room, messing up Jennie's hair as he went.

"Hey." She flung a hand at him, but he sidestepped her

easily and slipped into the hallway. She huffed at missing out on clobbering him, though she couldn't quite hide her smile. "I never did want a brother, you know!"

"Papa?" Ava walked in toward the table and began to secure Lenora in her highchair. "Why don't you come wrap up the left-over pork for you and Mama to take home?"

Leah glanced over at the empty cutting board. Hadn't they eaten it all?

"Sure, I can do that."

Ava grabbed her mother's hand. "And why don't you come meet up with him over here?"

And just like that, she was pressed up against Bryant, one wet, soapy hand against his chest, mistletoe hanging above them.

Unable to breathe.

"It's a Christmas law, you know. If there's mistletoe…" Ava's voice barely registered from somewhere behind her. "You have to kiss under it."

Leah closed her eyes. If she'd realized a second sooner what her daughter had been up to, her face wouldn't be on fire right now. She'd not kissed Bryant in so long…but to kiss him after all this time in front of their girls? Of course, half of her wanted to kiss him, but would that do her any good?

Yet God wouldn't want her to withdraw from him forever, so if feelings wouldn't come on their own, maybe—

Bryant's breath tickled her ear, sending a familiar thrill down her neck. "It's up to you."

She swallowed hard and opened her eyes, tried to nod, but her entire body was frozen.

His hold on her tightened, and her heart hammered.

Seconds ticked by. Did he not want to kiss her? They'd slept in bed together two nights in a row now, and he'd not once pressed his lips against hers. Was his desire for her extinguished whenever he saw the marks of his sins marring her face?

She clamped a hand around a fistful of his shirt. How could

she face a future of no more good memories with a man she couldn't live without—no matter how badly he'd wounded her?

She glanced over at Ava, whose face didn't appear as jolly as it had before. Then she looked back to Bryant. She forced herself to nod this time.

He leaned down, gave her a peck on the lips, then broke away.

"What was that?" A dishcloth hit her in the shoulder as Ava huffed. "Papa, that kiss wasn't worth the coal you're going to get in your stocking."

He cleared his throat and pulled farther away. "Well, there are rules governing the use of this plant. One being, you can't outshine the host and hostess under their own mistletoe."

Leah tried not to wilt. He'd made that excuse up for her. Even if this mistletoe had been theirs, she feared he'd not have kissed her any differently.

She was the reason for the disappointment coursing through her right now.

Bryant gently moved her to the side so he could get through the doorway, then headed for the table. Upon spotting the empty cutting board, likely realizing the pork had been a ruse, he took the board to the sink, then gave both his girls a kiss on their foreheads. "I need to head home."

And out of the kitchen he went. Why hadn't he asked to walk her home?

Leah took off her apron. "I'll go with him. And I'll work on reading your book tonight, Jennie. Maybe I'll be able to discuss it with you tomorrow."

"All right. Good night, Mama."

After the obligatory round of kisses, she rushed after Bryant. "Wait."

He stopped just outside the door and eyed her stiffly, but then came back in to grab her coat and held it open for her.

The second she stepped into the crisp evening air behind him, she clutched his sleeve. "Thank you for whatever it was you said to Oliver. He really tried with Lenora tonight. Nothing I've said has gotten him to do as much."

Though Bryant allowed her to thread her arm around his, he didn't draw her closer. "Sometimes a man needs another man to tell him bluntly how bad things are—or how bad they could become."

"Is that what happened to you? No one told you things weren't going to end well?"

"No, I was just an idiot, trying to avoid a blow to my pride. At least Oliver's getting practice in letting go of his pride now. Hopefully that'll help if he gets himself stuck in a rough spot in the future."

Moments passed, but he said no more.

She shuffled along beside him in the dense quiet of fresh snowfall, nerves jittering at the thought of bringing up what else had happened at Ava's. But not telling him would only save her from losing some of what Bryant had just succeeded in getting Oliver to lay down. "I know why you barely kissed me under the mistletoe."

He stiffened.

"To spare *my* pride." Hopefully that was all it was. For if he no longer found her attractive... "Uh, thank you for taking my feelings into consideration, but you don't have to..." She swallowed hard. "You don't have to wait for permission to kiss me if you want to."

He stopped, but didn't look at her, nor pull her closer. Just stared down the street toward the rising moon.

Was she wrong to think he was holding himself back? He'd always been the more affectionate one. What if he no longer wanted her like that? "You must have noticed that I've come to bed the last two nights, my trying to touch you more. You're allowed to touch me back."

He didn't move. "Are you saying this because you want me to, or because you're trying to trick yourself into liking me again?"

She staggered back a step. How had he figured that out?

"If you're talking about being intimate—"

His clipped voice startled her out of her thoughts.

"I'm not going to push you for that. Please—" His voice cracked. "Please don't try to force yourself into being intimate with me. Even if that means we'll never…"

She looked sharply up at him. Never?

He turned to face her, clamping his hands around her upper arms. "I know how things can be between us, and I don't want the counterfeit. And so you know, kissing you like that under the mistletoe was more for my sake than yours. If I allow myself too much of you, I'll be hard-pressed not to ask for more. But if you'd only do so out of duty…well, a young, single man might be willing to recklessly pursue that kind of pleasure, but I've known the love of a woman who's cared for me from the depths of her soul."

He released her, and her limbs grew heavy, her body having a sudden need to slump. His statement should've lifted the weight from her shoulders, but it hadn't.

"Besides," he spoke barely loud enough to hear. "If you're only pretending, how will I ever know if you've truly come to care for me again? So I'd rather wait, even if it's for years. That way, I can be certain that when you do come to me, you're doing so wholeheartedly."

Bryant tilted his face toward the stars that were just beginning to appear. "But if you're feeling better about…us…" The vulnerability that had stolen into his voice was heart-rending.

She put a hand on him, but only lightly. "I'm not sure I can say that…not yet."

He turned back to her. "I will care for you regardless of whether you ever can ever care for me again. Because I still love you. I always have and I always will, and not only because you're beautiful—"

She couldn't hold in her incredulous huff.

He grabbed her chin. "You've never scoffed before when I've said that."

She couldn't meet his eye. "I haven't ever looked or sounded like this before."

With his hand cupping the side of her face, his thumb slowly trailed down the puckered scar, which cut a line through her left eyebrow.

The gentle caress left her weak in the knees.

"There's a portion of your beauty that lies on the surface, yes." His soft voice puffed warm against her frozen cheek. "And that's been marred—I cannot lie. And I hate that I'm responsible for it. Yet, the part of your beauty that shines out from the inside has always enhanced what's been on the outside—and that's still all there."

She pulled away from him, shaking her head, forcing him to drop his hand. "With how I've treated you lately—?"

He pressed a finger to her lips. "You still care about others, Leah. And though you're having a hard time doing that with me right now, the way you care for our children, the way you humbly do the things everyone else overlooks—I've always loved that about you. I love *you*."

Though something inside her urged her to say those words back, words that months ago she would've repeated without thought, the knot in her throat wouldn't budge. Instead, she leaned into him, wrapping her arms around him, hoping to transfer some of those precious feelings into herself.

Though she was not the woman he claimed to see at this very moment, she wanted to be. She wanted to do what was best for others—including him.

He tucked her up against himself, and then pressed a single kiss atop her head. He rested his cheek against her hair. Despite his warmth, the chill of the wind blowing the snow around them soon caused her to shiver.

Bryant shifted. "It's too cold to stand out here any longer." And yet, a minute went by before he pulled himself from her and tucked her arm back around his, starting again for home. "Have you read Jennie's book yet?"

The sudden change of topic—to something that wouldn't fix what was broken between them—made her throat ache. But if he didn't want to talk any longer about that, she wouldn't press him since he didn't press her. "No, I haven't even finished the first chapter." Which was pretty awful, since the book wasn't even a hundred pages long. If only she could keep her mind on the words, but keeping focused proved difficult when her world felt upended.

"It's good. I think we should come up with ways to help her. Her stories make you realize what you have and that you should take none of it for granted." Gaining their porch, he stepped up to the front door, but didn't go in.

What was he waiting for? "You're wanting to do more than buy copies and give them to friends?"

"Maybe." He then opened the door and ushered her in. "I guess we can talk about ideas in the morning."

After hanging up her coat for her, he frowned at her when he realized she'd remained behind him.

He'd likely expected her to have already taken off, to claim some countertop was in desperate need of a midnight scrubbing.

She shifted her weight, having difficulty looking at him. "In light of what you said earlier about not wanting too much of me, would you rather I return to the guest room?"

"Please, no." His voice quavered. "I don't know how I'd survive if you took away what you've already given me—even if it's only for a few hours when you don't have to look at me."

"Bryant—"

He stopped her words with the back of his hand against her cheek. "Goodnight, sweetheart."

With that, he strode from the room and into the kitchen, a door shutting soon after. How long would he spend at the woodpile and tending to the firebox and coal stove? Likely a good amount of time with the way he'd just left.

She crossed over to the empty kitchen and frowned at the back door. This afternoon, as she'd stared at the Gethsemane glass, she'd resolved to do what was uncomfortable in hopes of doing what was best for them both, perhaps even giving her emotions a much-needed jouncing. But if that wasn't what Bryant wanted, what should she do now?

When he'd wrapped his arms around her and the girls at church this afternoon, whispered in her ear under the mistletoe, and held her in the moonlight-laced snow, she'd longed for what was missing, even though part of her still hesitated.

After marching up to the guest room, she searched her Bible for answers. Half an hour later, with the house much warmer than before, Bryant's heavy tread scuffled past her door. Down the hall, their door whined open, then shut. His footsteps didn't return. Laying aside her Bible, she readied for bed, then forged out into the hallway, but turned right back around to find her warm socks. Tomorrow, she'd pack up everything and drag it back down the hall.

By the time she entered their room, Bryant was snoring softly.

Slipping in beside him, she pressed herself closer than she'd allowed herself last night. Surely soon she'd be able to tell him she loved him with just as much meaning as he'd put into those words earlier—to feel again what she now wished she still did.

Deep down, she still loved him, but to feel *that* way again…

Would those feelings lie dormant until she forced them to engage? Was it naïve to expect the resentment and bitterness she'd nursed for half a year to fade away? She moved to press a kiss to his neck. Maybe if she warmed him up.

But then flashes of the nights she'd lain in this spot, sleeping in her clothes because she'd been too sore to undress, the days she'd sold cherished items to buy food, and the afternoons he'd not been there to hold her when she'd been in pain thwarted her attempt to stoke that momentary spark of desire.

With a huff, she rolled back and stared up at the ceiling. Whatever passion she'd just fanned into existence had sputtered out.

He deserved what he'd asked for—a woman who desired him out of love—not in search of it.

Making no attempt to wipe away the tears dripping down her cheeks, she spent the next hour listening to Bryant's breathing while praying for a new heart, a heart that overflowed with desire for her husband.

CHAPTER NINE

Jennie handed Bryant another length of twine as they sat by the fireplace, wrapping the presents he'd helped her buy earlier. Only a few more days and Christmas would be over, and his sweet daughter would be heading back to Chicago. He turned toward her, waiting for another piece of twine. "I finished your book."

She continued to pull string through her fingers, measuring by feel, staring somewhere to the left of him. With how she'd tilted her chin, he could tell she was waiting for him to say more.

"I thought it was well done and insightful." He wanted to reach over and sweep back the dark hair that had fallen over her eyes, but he'd learned yesterday she no longer appreciated him 'babying' her. She wanted to appear just as she was, for she couldn't have parents following her around at all times, making sure she looked presentable.

She cut the next piece of twine and handed it to him. "Do you think anyone will buy it?"

He shrugged. "They should, and I hope for your sake, they will. But a publisher should know—"

"I'm going to sell it myself." She nodded decisively. "A few of my friends from the blind school attempted to get a publisher, but no one succeeded. A press printed it for them though, and they've gone around to different towns selling their books. So that's what I'm going to do, along with singing guest solos at churches."

Bryant's hands froze against the Christmas package he'd been working on. His girl intended to travel alone? "Uh, no." He shook his head harder than she was shaking hers and repeated, "No."

"Papa—"

"Who's going to protect you?" She had no idea how enticing a vulnerable, pretty woman could be to riffraff.

"I plan on hiring someone at each place, who can—"

"That won't do. You don't know people in every town."

"I can ask at the churches—"

"And how are you going to get to the church without someone taking you there? And that someone might be—"

"I'm old enough to choose how I live my life." She folded her hands in her lap and sighed. "I've lived away from you almost longer than I've lived with you."

She might as well have stabbed him in the heart. "That's because—"

"I'm not blaming you, Papa." She raised her hand to stop any further contest. "I'm grateful you sent me to school. It was far better than staying here, stuck in a corner."

"Honey—"

"Don't take that as chastisement. I understand no one knew what to do with me, that you were trying to protect me, and that sending me to school was because you didn't want to see me stuck in the corner any longer—and I'm not. I'm ready to go out into the world, and the school gave me the ability to do so."

She might be ready, but he wasn't, not one iota. What to say that wouldn't dampen her courage, or relegate her back to the corner, yet get her to see how dangerous this idea was.

God...

His heart thumped. He immediately knew the answer to his unfinished prayer.

He'd already promised he'd do whatever God told him to do to support his wife financially—but he'd received no peace about staying. However, he'd been unable to fathom how leaving would be a good thing.

Now he knew. Leah didn't need support, but their girls did —which had been Leah's exact objection to leaving Armelle. She hadn't wanted to abandon Ava. So if their oldest needed Leah, and Jennie was going out all alone…

He hung his head.

He'd told God he'd lay down his life for his wife, but he'd do so for his daughters as well. Surely God wouldn't want him to leave the most vulnerable member of his family to fend for herself just because he wished things were better between him and his wife. He'd told Oliver they ought to strive to be men that sacrificed the future they'd hoped for to do their best by those they loved.

Distance couldn't stop him from sending Leah whatever money he could spare or from writing letters. "I'll do it."

Jennie tipped her head. "Do what?"

"Take you around the country. Help you sell your books. For as long as you want."

She laughed. "Mama couldn't live without you."

He grimaced. If only that were true. "She'll manage just fine, but you might not. I'll do whatever it takes to help you live the life you want."

"Papa…"

"Within reason, of course. No illegal activities." How had he ever been so sure of himself that he'd gambled her tuition to save his pride? "We'll both work hard, you'll sell a lot of books, and I'll scare off every young man within five miles of you."

She grinned. "I'm not sure I want you to work too hard at doing that. But I can't take you from Mama that long.

Depending on how well I do, I might travel for a year, or even longer."

"That's fine. If your mother changes her mind about staying here, she could join us."

Staring off into the unseen distance, Jennie chewed on her lip.

She'd be unable to come up with an argument to convince him he wasn't needed. If she didn't suddenly marry someone within the week—and she better not—he'd be by her side the next time she got on a train.

"I'm not certain my book sales will be enough to provide for us both."

"I can do odd jobs." He squirmed. "You may not have realized my felony conviction has made it difficult for me to find work. I have to move to have any real chance at gainful employment."

She sat with her head cocked, as if she could hear something in the silence. "Things are that bad between you and Mama?"

How she could've "heard" that, he didn't know, but he couldn't deny it. "Yes."

"I'm sorry."

"You've nothing to be sorry about, sweetheart." In fact—he swallowed a suddenly formed lump—she might be the biggest ray of sunshine in his life right now, a reason to get up every morning, someone who wanted him…loved him. Plus, spending time getting to know his youngest who'd been, as she'd said, away from them longer than she'd been with them would be a joy. So much of her childhood had been stunted after her accident, and agreeing to send her off to school had been one of the hardest decisions of his life.

"I don't intend to be here much past Christmas." For some reason, Jennie had lowered her voice. "I've got to get back to Chicago and make a deal with a printer and then vacate my quarters. Are you sure you want to leave so quickly?"

"I've already told your mother I can't stay long." Should he beg her to reconsider leaving? But if she said no again, he might be crushing Jennie's hopes as well. "I can pack up as soon as you're ready to go."

"Where're you planning to go?" Leah's voice sliced through the room.

Bryant's heart jolted. He turned to face his wife, her face screwed up as if she'd smelled something unpleasant.

She took a step forward, her jaw hard, her shoulders cocked. "You're leaving already?"

He blew out a shaky breath. "This isn't something I've kept from you, honey. If I've any chance at finding a job, I have to leave. More importantly, Jennie needs me—she's going to sell her story by traveling the nation and needs protection. And as you've said, you have to stay because Ava needs you."

"But Oliver needs guidance."

"And there are men here who could give him that. Jennie doesn't have anyone."

"Why not come with us, Mama?"

Jennie's question sucked all the wind out of his lungs. He forced himself not to mouth 'please' to Leah.

His wife pulled over a chair and took Jennie's hands in her own. "Why not stay here with us? I could use you in the laundry."

"I think my story needs to be told, Mama."

"I agree." Though he'd done his best to never disagree with his wife in front of the girls, this was Jennie's future they were talking about. "And she's just like her mother, insisting she can do things without help, even when she needs it."

Leah narrowed her eyes at him. "I *can* do things without help. I've done it for months. If it weren't for the banker keeping me from buying—"

"Now hold on." He held up a hand, already regretting his choice to talk in front of Jennie. Why bother trying to convince

Leah to come along when buying the laundry was still foremost on her mind? "Why don't you sell the house?"

Leah jerked back. "The house?"

"You were living in the laundry apartment when I returned, so what good does this house do you? Buy the laundry outright from the bank with the proceeds from the house's sale. Whatever you have left will keep you afloat during times the laundry doesn't bring in enough."

She sat blinking at him. "You mean you're not coming back at all?"

He broke his gaze from hers to stare at his clasped hands. His heart began to pound, and he looked over at his daughter. Her head was cocked in a manner unique to her, and her eyes roamed about as if she could see. Was her heart trembling like his own? Worried over how his answer would affect them all?

But he couldn't let his daughter go out in the world at the mercy of whoever met her first at the train station. God would protect her, yes, but surely He'd do so through her father. "Jennie's not sure how long she wants to do this, so I can't say when we'll come back. But when we do, I'm certain Ava will let Jennie stay with her."

Leah wrung a section of her skirt in her hands. "But you were so proud of this house."

He shrugged. "Who cares about the house?"

"I do."

"Why?" He pushed himself off the floor. "You've told me you don't need *me*, and I have nothing else to offer."

Before either of them said anything more they might regret, he left for his room. Tomorrow, he'd give the banker the permission he needed to allow Leah to proceed with whatever business endeavors she wanted to pursue.

Shutting their bedroom door behind him, he forced himself to breathe deeply so as not to tear up. He had returned to Armelle believing God had wanted him to fix his marriage, but maybe God had brought him home to assist Jennie in sharing her gifts and talents with the world. He'd told Leah he'd not push her to soften toward him before she was ready, but maybe he'd have to wait from a distance, woo her through letters, give her more time to heal.

Though leaving while his marriage was still in shambles was not what he wanted, it seemed God was asking him to do just that.

But for how long?

Please, God, don't let it be forever. And yet, Thy will be done.

CHAPTER TEN

Soft, fat snowflakes brushed the laundry's windows and piled up on the sill, making the afternoon silence even more hushed. Leah returned her cold iron to the stove, but didn't take up the hot one. She glanced at the door though it was unlikely many would venture out now, even if it was Christmas Eve and their best suit and gown awaited them on the counter.

Of course, she didn't care who came in if it wasn't Bryant, though he surely wasn't coming either. Nor had he come yesterday or the day before. Once he'd decided to help Jennie sell her books, he'd not returned to work at the laundry.

Somehow, she felt even lonelier than when he'd been in prison.

He really was leaving.

She sniffled, but then stamped her foot to stop herself. She had no right to be sniffling. He'd told her he had to go. She'd told him she had to stay. And if he didn't go, she'd think less of him for letting Jennie go off into the world alone and unprotected.

The door bell jangled, and Leah spun so fast, she pulled something in her neck.

It was only Miss McGill.

Leah held in her groan and massaged the pain now pulsing below her ear.

"It's cold out there. Brrr." Gwen rubbed her arms encased in a fur-lined coat Leah fought not to be jealous of. The white wool was trimmed in the softest-looking gray fur. Though it probably wouldn't look as good on her since Gwen was still young and unscarred.

Leah left the shirt she was ironing to meet Gwen at the counter. "What brings you out in this weather?" Or for that matter, to the laundry at all. Had she ever seen Gwen here? Though the young lady's father had devastated his family, Gwen's brother seemed to be managing their money well enough to keep their fine house and staff.

"I was hoping you might possess some magic."

She gave her a slight smile. "I'm afraid no stores in Armelle can offer you that."

"I'd hoped Miss Stillwa—I mean, Mrs. Key had left you with some secret formula for getting out stubborn stains." Gwen pulled out a gorgeous emerald dress from a large bag. "I wanted to wear this to the Christmas program, but these black marks on the hem will not budge. I simply cannot wear this in front of Mr. Parks's nephew, you know the one who comes up from Laramie? No woman wants to make a bad impression on a man like that."

Leah shook her head. "I thought you'd set your cap for Mr. Wright."

Gwen fluttered her eyelashes. "A girl without a ring on her finger should keep her options open—especially for someone like Andrew Parks, who is dashedly handsome and part owner of a railway. Do you think you could get the stain out before you close?"

"If you braved the snow for this, I suppose I could try, but I can't promise anything. I've not the flair for mixing chemicals like Mrs. Key."

Gwen put a hand on Leah's. "Oh, do try your best. Otherwise, Mr. Parks will see me in my red dress two years in a row, and that won't do for catching a man's eye."

Without knowing what possessed her, Leah set her free hand atop Gwen's and stared straight into her cheery glibness—it had to be fake, right?

Gwen's eyebrows rose, but she didn't pull away. Something intelligent flickered in her blue eyes, which normally seemed jolly, yet blank. "Was there something you needed, Mrs. Whitsett?"

Leah looked away for a second, but then pulled in a huge draught of air. What other woman in Armelle could sympathize with the betrayal she'd incurred? Gwen's father had been the mastermind of the crimes that had adversely affected them both. "Have you been able to forgive your father yet?"

Gwen's hand tensed between Leah's. After looking Leah in the eye for a moment then glancing toward the door, all tension seemed to drain out of her, and then her expression changed, almost as if she'd aged five years in a moment. "Pastor Lawrence has said many times that love is a decision. A promise to act. Not a feeling. At least, the kind of love God asks of us. So I figured since God commands us to forgive as well, the same could be said of that. So I decided whenever I felt unforgiving, I'd act as if I wasn't. Or at least ignore the compulsion to say or do anything to the contrary." She gave Leah a weak smile. "Prayer seems to help, too. I'm not sure I can say I feel as if I've forgiven my father, but I'm going to say that I have."

Such mature insight from a woman many would describe as flighty. Only weeks ago, Leah had figured Gwen would be the one needing her guidance rather than the other way around. "I'm impressed."

Gwen shrugged. "I'm not certain you should be. I can't say how I'll feel when I see him again."

Leah glanced out the window. The snow had stopped. "I'm finding that having Bryant home is more difficult than I'd imagined. I hope you don't struggle as much as I have when your father returns."

"Oh, I don't intend to still be here when he comes back—if he has the audacity to do so."

Did others think it was audacious of Bryant to return? He'd told her finding employment was difficult, but was there more to it?

"And it's different for me." Gwen pulled her hand from Leah's and began to twist a loose thread on the tablecloth folded beside her. "My father may have provided for my needs, but he never gave me anything out of love, really. He dressed me to the nines and let me furnish our house—more so to reflect well on himself than to make me happy. No one has ever mistaken my father for a loving parent."

Gwen shook her head slightly. "Anyone who was at the trial heard how my father had Bryant pinned in a corner. And everyone knows how much your husband loves you. His mistakes may have been rooted in selfishness, but that isn't the whole of his character. However, ever since my mother died... there's been nothing left inside my father that cares about anyone other than himself."

Leah recaptured Gwen's hand. "If it's any consolation, everyone I know marvels that you and Bo are as kind and well-adjusted as you are."

The young woman huffed. "Kind? Bo maybe. I just keep to myself."

Keep to herself? The girl who'd flirted with nearly every man who stepped foot in Armelle?

Gwen smiled brightly, and Leah tightened her hold before Gwen pulled away. "Do you not think people will think us weak-willed for forgiving them too quickly? If I start talking about Bryant again like I used to, telling others what a good husband he is or how much I love him, don't you think I'd appear gullible and stupid?"

"Mrs. Tate and her ilk might think so, but for those who

want the best for you? None of us want to see you miserable just to make sure Bryant is. Besides, he did what he did trying to protect his family—my father wasn't thinking about Bo or me."

"You may be the only one who thinks Bryant's motivations had any merit. No one here will hire him, so he has to leave town."

"I'm sorry to hear that." Gwen gave Leah's hand a squeeze. "We'll miss you, but I understand."

She'd so easily assumed she'd go with Bryant that Leah had to look away.

Gwen blew out an exasperated breath. "If I'm ever going to get married, I'll have to leave, too. The good Lord knows I've flirted with every eligible man here before my father was sent to prison, so there's no chance I can win any of them over now. And if Mr. Wright does come back and marry me, he couldn't stay here and be taken seriously. For what it's worth though, I'd be thrilled to have you and Bryant walking around town, snuggled up like you once were. I've always wanted the kind of love you have."

Had.

Leah winced at the bitterness that colored her thought. Especially since *she* was more responsible for the coolness between them than Bryant. The other night, he'd made it clear he still loved her. And everything he'd done since his return proved him to be the man she knew. His deception last year had been the aberration, his criminal actions driven somewhat by an attempt to protect his girls, which was what he'd always done— was still doing.

Gwen's gentle pat pulled her from her thoughts.

"Don't worry about my dress. I'll find something else to wear. Have a merry Christmas."

Leah pulled herself together to wish her a merry Christmas as well.

Once Gwen left, Leah stared at her irons, having no desire to pick one back up.

Bryant was right. She'd talked him up so much over the years that she'd begun to love a man who didn't exist, causing the real man to fear he'd lose her if he couldn't live up to her ideal.

Though he'd failed her and could do so again, he was attempting to do what God wanted of him. What was more ideal than that?

Therefore, she too must do what she ought. As Gwen had said, God didn't ask His followers to feel like forgiving or loving their enemies. For who feels like loving an enemy?

And Bryant was certainly not her enemy.

God might not demand feeling, but He did demand action. And a man, who tried to put his love into action—even if he did so disastrously at times, was worthy of forgiveness.

CHAPTER ELEVEN

Pastor Lawrence began the Christmas evening program with a prayer that echoed through the sanctuary. "God, thank you for the good news of peace that came wrapped in swaddling clothes hundreds of years ago that we honor here tonight. May our praises be welcome, may our joy be refreshed, may we be humbled by…"

As he continued, Leah thanked God that a hint of that peace had returned to her. After her talk with Gwen yesterday, Leah had gone to bed hopeful. This morning at Ava's house, celebrating Christmas with a sleeping baby in her arms had buoyed her hope that God would help her regain joy with time if she followed Him in obedience.

Out of the corner of her eye, she watched her husband, who'd closed his eyes, praying along with the congregation.

He'd handed out gifts this morning. As usual, he'd carved everyone an ornament. Hers had been a simple heart.

She'd not made him anything, and he'd acted as if he hadn't noticed.

She knew what he wanted most, but until yesterday, she'd been uncertain she could give him that.

Finished with the prayer, Pastor Lawrence invited them to

contemplate the meaning of Christmas in silence, and Leah thought back on this morning's message, which had seemed tailor-made for her. The simple, but often taken for granted truth that God loved mankind so much He made good on His promises, even though people failed Him.

She'd promised Bryant to love him through the good and the bad, deserved or undeserved. Choosing feelings over vows hadn't improved her life one bit.

Across the aisle, Corinne was snuggled up to Nolan. Married a few months ago, their story was a true representation of God's love rescuing mankind from desperation and offering them abundant life.

How does my marriage demonstrate God's love?

Right now, it didn't. But it wasn't too late. God had been angry at the world plenty of times before Jesus came. Never had He pretended sin hadn't hurt the relationship. Yet He chose to sacrifice Himself out of love for the sake of reconciliation.

"Mrs. Whitsett?"

Her head jolted up at the pastor's insistent whisper.

His eyes were wide, and he tilted his head toward the piano.

"Oh!" She stood and hastened her way up to play. If she didn't rein in her thoughts, she might be the one responsible for mucking up Ava's hopes for the perfect nativity scene.

Bryant escorted Jennie to the piano and together, Leah and her youngest started a reverent rendition of "Christ was Born on Christmas Day." However, when Spencer gained the stage, nearly prancing with excitement as Jacob hooked him to the rope, the aura of reverence thinned as a smattering of chuckles broke out throughout the audience.

The pastor moved to the side of the platform where he would read the Christmas story, and Ava and her family came in from the side door to arrange themselves in the manger scene.

When Spencer took flight, several oohs and aahs and one loud gasp—from Mrs. Tate, no doubt—interrupted the pastor's reading.

Too bad she had to keep her eyes glued to the music as the rope creaked against the rafters. Spencer's smile was probably brighter than the lamp lit star.

After letting the last chord dampen to silence, she swiveled on her bench to listen to the rest of the reading and almost choked trying to suppress a laugh.

Spencer was certainly hanging from the rafters, but his smile was more a grimace. His squirmy attempts to adjust himself in the harness made him look more like a crippled goose than an angel in flight.

A flying Christmas angel was likely to be a short-lived tradition.

The pastor turned the page in his Bible. "And this *shall be* a sign unto you; Ye shall find the babe wrapped in swaddling clothes, lying in a manger."

Leah turned to see Lenora, and this time failed to hold in her amusement. Her granddaughter was struggling to sit up in her straw bed, and Oliver was pushing her back down only to have "baby Jesus" practically sneer at him. After Oliver's third attempt to furtively press her back, Lenora let out a very un-Jesus-like grunt of frustration.

The whole church burst into laughter, startling Lenora. She began to cry big dollops of tears.

Without any prodding, Oliver picked her up and did an awkward job of patting her on the back while she fussed.

Leah put a hand against her chest. What a balm to her heart to see—

"*Woof!*" Mickey growled at something at the back of the church and started to go after whatever it was. Ava lunged for the old dog and when pulling him back, tore off some "wool."

Upon being thwarted, Mickey quickly changed his mind and jumped back into Ava's lap, nearly knocking her over with a kiss to her face.

The entire church erupted in a fresh bout of laughter as the

"Virgin Mary" tried to keep an overeager "sheep" from licking her on the lips.

The pastor plowed through the end of the story, often clearing his throat in a desperate attempt to keep himself together. The moment the last verse was read, Nolan called for his dog from the pews, and Ava audibly sighed. She turned to her husband, and when she glimpsed her daughter burrowed into Oliver's neck, her scowl immediately disappeared and her face practically glowed.

Despite the craziness, this little Christmas pageant turned out better than Leah had thought it would. She stood to guide Jennie back to their seat as the pastor led the congregation in an a cappella rendition of "Silent Night."

Leah weaved around the deacons passing out the candles and helped her youngest slide onto the family pew. Instead of sitting next to Jennie though, Leah squished her way past her daughter's knees and stumbled past Bryant to sit on his other side. He gave her a strange look but handed her a candle.

Once their candles were lit, Leah passed the flame to the people in front of them, then wriggled her free hand beneath Bryant's and threaded her fingers through his.

He glanced down at their hands clasped together, then looked up at her. She couldn't help but smile at the adorable wrinkle in his brow.

His expression relaxed. "You're beautiful in candlelight," he whispered.

She bit her lip to keep from countering his compliment, gave him a wink, then turned to listen to the last verse of "Silent Night."

As was tradition, after the song ended, they all filed out of the church wordlessly with their candles, in contemplation of the Love that came down to bring joy to the world.

Outside, Jennie stopped the moment they'd stepped off the porch, causing Leah to nearly trip over her.

Jennie somehow grabbed her faster than Bryant had. "I'm

sorry, Mama. I was stopping to tell you I've decided to stay with Ava again tonight." She turned her head slightly. "Ava?"

"I'm right here." Her sister walked over and took Jennie's elbow. "We'd be happy to have you again."

Leah swallowed. This would be the second night Jennie would stay with her sister. There weren't many days left of Jennie's visit.

Oliver walked up slowly, his eyes not on his wife or Jennie but Lenora's little face smooshed against his arm. Lenora looked sweet with her squished cheeks and slack mouth bathed in moonlight. Seemingly reluctantly, he passed his blanketed bundle over to Ava. "I'll get the buggy."

The girls followed after him, leaving Leah and Bryant to exchange hushed goodbyes with neighbors and promises of prayers for safe travel to those leaving town by lantern light.

After a quiet conversation with the stagecoach driver, Bryant returned to her side. "You ready to get out of the cold?"

She nodded, but when he started off in front of her, she frowned.

Was he not even going to try to hold her hand after she'd held his during the last song?

After passing several houses, it seemed Bryant was content— or maybe resigned—to walk home in silence. With how often she'd avoided him since his return and their argument the other night, she'd probably kept him from hoping for anything more than not fighting until he left with Jennie.

She caught up and took his hand. She'd have to change the pattern. Though he glanced down with surprise again, he didn't pull away.

"I was thinking the other day, there's nearly seven months of your life I know nothing about. I know it's my fault, since I never asked, and maybe you don't want to talk about it, but I'd like to know. I can't imagine it was easy."

Many minutes passed, with nothing but the sound of their feet crunching in old snow.

She *had* asked her question out loud, hadn't she?

About a block from home, he sighed. "Prison was simply a series of endless blank days."

"So it wasn't that bad?"

"Oh, it was bad. Every morning, I woke up thinking you'd gone to the kitchen to start breakfast as always, then within seconds, I realized you hadn't been beside me all night, or the night before, nor would you be there for any of the nights ahead."

Her heart did a sad flop.

"What made that worse was knowing you weren't doing well. Not only were you not writing me, but when Jake visited, he shied away from answering any of my questions about you."

"Jake went to see you?" She'd only known he'd escorted him to the prison.

"Sometime in June. He was worried about me."

"Worried?"

"About what I'd do to myself." His voice was so hushed, she'd barely heard him.

"You mean…?" She clasped her throat. "Jake thought you'd—?"

He squeezed her hand. "I didn't. I'm still here."

She tried to squeeze him back, but couldn't. What right did she have to comfort him now? How heartless had she been for him to believe he'd not be missed?

After she'd finally regained consciousness days after the disastrous night she'd endured with Celia and the rustlers, she'd flirted with fatal thoughts herself. The first time she'd taken a good look in the mirror, noting how her body would forever now be in her way; the hours she'd grimaced through the pain of simply breathing; the weeks she'd ruminated over her husband's betrayal and working up the courage to face the town—often, she'd wished she'd never woken up.

She'd been in a dark place for months. Then one day, Jacob had borne the brunt of her tirade against Bryant when Jacob had visited unannounced. Had he come over to tell her about Bryant then? Was that why he'd not told her about his worries?

Over the next few months, she'd had Annie and Corrine and the doctor's wife to encourage her to get back on her feet. Ava, Jennie, Lenora, and Celia to live for.

Bryant, however, didn't even have a kind letter from her to give him any hope for the future.

What if he'd killed himself and she'd lost him forever?

Her throat grew tight and her eyes stung. She couldn't have stopped the tears if she'd tried.

"What's wrong?" Bryant slowed and pulled her close, the warmth of his body barely registering against the ice that had encased her heart for so long.

"I didn't know. I was so hurt. I didn't care. I should've—"

"Shhh." He pressed a finger to her lips. "Don't blame yourself for what I faced. That was all my doing. You're not responsible for—"

"Don't make excuses for me." She pulled away from him. "I've done wrong, too—as much as you have, or maybe more, because it seems you did everything out of a desire to protect me. I only wanted to lash out at you."

His brows drew together, as if unsure how to respond.

"In an odd sort of way, it felt good to be mad—to…to hate." She crossed her arms tight against her middle, not letting herself return to his embrace. "Like too much sugar, it feels good for a while until you notice the sickening feeling building up on the inside."

He reached for her, but she stepped back.

She held up her hand. "Before all this, I'd found it easy to do what God wanted. I've had some hard times, but nothing which had hurt me so deeply, so badly."

She spun and marched toward the house. "What a fool I've been over the years, advising others how to follow God during rough times when I could fail like this."

Bryant's footsteps were steady beside her, his presence, like always, watchful, but never pushy.

Hot tears rolled down her icy cheeks, and she smeared them away. Bryant had stuck to his vows, chosen to love her, though she'd abandoned him to face the worst six months of his life alone. Even sticking with her when she'd continued to punish him after he'd finished paying his debt to society.

From now on—as Gwen had suggested—if an unforgiving or vengeful thought crossed her mind, she'd make herself think the opposite. If she didn't choose love, she'd likely lose herself— and she'd definitely lose him. Tomorrow, she might not wake up as remorseful as she felt now, but she'd not let those feelings rule her.

How could she start off tomorrow in the right direction? What did a loving, forgiving wife do? She released all her pent up air in a rush. "In the morning, would you prefer I make doughnuts or that sausage and egg dish you like?"

After a step or two, she realized his footfalls no longer sounded alongside her. She turned.

Even from several feet away, she could see the tears glistening on his face in the moonlight.

"You mean...?" His rough voice caught.

She nodded slightly. She'd no longer force him to fend for himself. As she'd done for twenty years before this, she'd be waiting at the breakfast table, pray with him before they ate, kiss him before they parted for the day.

"I uh..." A long puffy cloud of frothy air filled the space between them as Bryant fidgeted. "I think I'd prefer you not to worry about breakfast at all."

Why would he reject her olive branch? Oh. Bryant's eyes were filled with something akin to hope. "You mean, you want me to stay by your side until you wake up?"

His nod was subtle, his body rigid as if bracing for rejection.

She looked back toward town. "I suppose anyone who wants

to drop off their laundry in the morning can wait a little longer."

He covered the space between them and slid his thumb from the corner of her mouth to the underside of her jaw. "Thank you."

She nodded, and he planted a kiss atop her head before tucking her in close. For a second, she held herself stiffly against him, but couldn't do so for long. A spiral of warmth surged through her as she relaxed against him. Burrowing into his side, her frozen limbs stopped complaining as they walked the rest of the way home together.

How she'd missed hearing his heart, being guided by his steady arm.

Seemed doing something she ought to do, though she didn't *feel* like it, hadn't been so bad after all. In fact, she couldn't wait to see how she'd feel in the morning.

Tomorrow would be a better day than today. And even if it didn't feel like it, she'd make it so.

CHAPTER TWELVE

Bryant stepped out of the mercantile and flipped up the collar of his coat. He should've put on more layers before venturing out to get what he and Jennie needed to travel next week.

Across the street, his girls were safe and warm behind the seamstress's ice-encrusted window. Ava had gifted her sister a couple new dresses for Christmas, insisting it'd help Jennie's image as a saleswoman. Ava could never resist dressing up her little sister, especially since Jennie trusted her to pick the styles she'd like.

He'd hoped to see Leah at the fitting, but from what he could see through the window, she still hadn't appeared.

Though he was freezing, he didn't welcome the cruel sort of heat that filled him. He'd initially been happy this morning, waking up with his wife at his side. As promised, she hadn't gotten up before dawn to cook breakfast, but she'd fidgeted long enough he knew she hadn't wanted to be there. Though she'd allowed him to keep his arm around her as he dozed through the first hour of daybreak, he'd not pushed for anything more.

Last night, he'd thought they'd turned a corner, but maybe not. Either that or Leah's early-rising habit was too ingrained for her to lie still and soak up the morning. As soon as the clock had chimed eight, he'd kissed her forehead and freed her to go start breakfast.

But when he'd entered the kitchen a half hour later, he'd found biscuits, jam, and a pitcher of milk. No Leah.

He sighed, his breath a frosty cloud in front of him. She used to tell him every single plan she had for the upcoming day over breakfast. Then they would pray, and he'd kiss her good-bye. He'd been looking forward to that this morning. But once again, she'd left him in the dark as to her plans and whereabouts.

He shook his head at his disappointment. Six months in prison had forced her to get along without him, and perhaps she'd gotten used to that. Or maybe she subconsciously believed he'd abandon her again and was going about life in a way that wouldn't hurt so much when he did. Of course, he *was* leaving, but not because he'd failed her or even because he wanted to, but because he had to.

Looking both ways before crossing the street, he forced himself not to slump as he walked. When he opened the seamstress's door, a fiery blast of warmth smote him in the face. Goodness, it was like an oven in here.

"Hey, Papa." Ava gave him a big grin as Jennie stood dutifully with her arms widespread while the seamstress took measurements.

"Hey, pumpkin." He scanned the room but only saw empty chairs. "I'd thought your mother would've wanted to help with the dresses."

"We invited her," Jennie said, shrugging. "But she hasn't come. Did you get everything we need?"

"Yes." Other than her mother's presence. Surely Leah hadn't been so desperate to leave his side this morning that she'd headed straight to the laundry, but where else would she be? Or maybe the day after Christmas was the busiest day of the year for a washerwoman. "I'll go see if I can find your mother. She'll at least want to know what colors you're picking so she can get you a few hats from the new milliner."

Jennie sighed audibly. "I don't need hats."

He gave her a lopsided grin. "I have a feeling you'll get them anyway."

The seamstress pulled a pin from her mouth. "I saw a divine yellow one with fake grapes draping off the side—oh!" She looked to Ava. "I have some yellow muslin. With Jennie's dark hair and…"

Bryant backed out of the store, knowing he was no longer needed. Maybe he'd be needed at the laundry. Perhaps after Christmas dinners, everyone rushed in first thing to get stains removed before they set.

When he entered the laundry, a dark-headed woman with sharp features stood behind the counter, her arms full of linens.

"*Guten morgen.* How can I help you?"

He cocked his head, trying to place the woman or think of a family in the area that had such a heavy accent other than the Volkmanns. "I was looking for Mrs. Whitsett."

"I work here now."

He blinked. "You do?"

Her face lit up. "Oh yes, it was *Gott*'s blessing. I use my last moneys to buy ze children an apple for Christmas, and now I have zis."

His heart gave a slow, hopeful thump. Had Leah given the laundry away? Could that mean…?

The woman pointed to three young boys he'd not noticed playing jacks. "Now, we have a room to stay where it is dry when it rains, money to make, and food to buy when I get pay. It is a very much blessing. How can I do for you, sir? I will do more than Mrs. Whitsett, please."

"You'll do more than Mrs. Whitsett?"

She nodded emphatically. "She will teach me what I do not

know, and then I will work very hard. You will be happy with my work."

So this woman was an employee? The bubble inside his chest deflated. The milliner had told him Leah had been looking for help—and since he'd be leaving next week, Leah would need someone.

He closed his eyes. After last night, he'd thought about asking Jennie to postpone their trip to give Leah a chance to change her mind, but perhaps he'd only be delaying the inevitable.

"Mister?"

He opened his eyes, sorry to deny this woman work since her face was lit with such anticipation. "I don't have any laundry, I was just looking for my... uh, Mrs. Whitsett."

"Oh." She frowned and looked toward the snow-spattered window. "She is not here right now. Maybe later when she come you can see her?"

He nodded as if he planned to return and backed out into the cold.

Likely best to go home and wait there rather than wander around looking for his wife. For what would he even say to her when he saw her? He had started to hope she'd come with him, but he'd been too optimistic.

Heading down the boardwalk, he didn't get far before his gaze gravitated to the movement of a figure in his peripheral vision— Leah had just left the seamstress's shop. She stopped at the edge of the boardwalk, tucked in her scarf, then pressed a hand to her hip.

So much for going home. Part of him wanted to go offer his arm. The other part simply froze.

Gingerly she stepped into the street, papers tucked under her arm. Her limp was more pronounced than usual, her face more beautiful. The cold wind amplified the roses in her cheeks and tugged at the pins in her hair, loosening her dark locks to frame her dear face.

He drank in the sight of her, for he might not see her again for a long time.

Upon spotting him, Leah limped straight over. After crossing the street, she took the papers out from under her arm. "I went to talk to Bo McGill this morning, and he sent me to the Volkmanns. They might be interested in the house if they can handle the payments. Mr. Rice is offering more, but I'd rather see it go to Charles and Lavinia since they'd hoped to have her mother moved in already."

She continued, a little winded. "Charles plans to add on to his house again once the snow clears, but they already have such a small yard. It'd be a shame to lose more of it when they've got so many children. What do you think?"

Seeing her go forward with selling their house so quickly hit him hard. The house would be perfect for the Volkmanns, but then, where was Leah going to stay? "I just talked to the lady at the laundry. I thought she said she was going to live in the upstairs apartment. So are you moving in with Ava?"

"No." She gave him a look, which usually meant he'd been caught not paying attention. "I'm going with you."

"You are?" His chest nearly caved in on itself.

"Yes, Mr. Rice has agreed to lease the laundry to Mrs. Gerwig, the Volkmanns should take the house, and I'm going with you."

"But what about being a grandmother? Helping Ava?"

She glanced over her shoulder toward the seamstress's shop. "I talked to the girls. Jennie's fine with us coming back whenever we can, four times a year if possible."

Since Jennie wanted to visit all the big cities, that would take a lot of traveling. As much as he wanted Leah to come… "Are you sure? Wouldn't your hip—?"

"I can't imagine it'd be any more difficult than standing in the laundry all day. Plus, I could probably sit some while Jennie's selling books."

He swallowed hard against the hope he didn't want to squash back down.

She tilted her head. "Don't you want me to come?"

"Of course! I'll always want you with me, but I don't want you to resent me any more than you already do. When I'd first asked you to leave with me, I was hoping to settle somewhere, but with Jennie wanting us to travel, I hadn't thought it through. You—"

"I don't resent you, Bryant." She took a small step forward and looked up at him, her eyes intense. "I love you."

The wintry air he'd sucked in couldn't keep his head from swimming. Did she really mean that or had she only said that because she thought she ought to?

She took another step closer and ran a hand down his arm. "I love you so much, that no one else has ever had the power to hurt me like you do. But I'd never believed you would, so when you did, I broke. Especially when I realized how you could hurt me again and I was afraid you'd do so."

"One day, I hope to get back into your good graces. I'll never again—"

"Not one day, Bryant. Today."

Today? "What do you mean?"

"That I miss you. That I forgive you. That I trust you. Right now. I choose to."

"Truly?" He ran a hand through his hair to keep from snatching her up, his arms literally shaking with the need to have her closer. Could he still be dreaming? Perhaps he'd fallen asleep with his arms around her, and any moment he'd awaken and she'd not be—

Soft arms slipped around him under his coat, and Leah's warmth was as undeniable as the freezing snowflake hitting the back of his neck.

She tilted her head back to look at him. "I'm ready to love you again with my whole heart—still afraid, mind you, but I'm miserable without you, inside and out. I've not been a fun person to be around for a while, and I'm sorry. Forgive me?"

The dark heaviness that had weighed him down for more than a year melted away like the snow upon her face. He swiped a snowflake off her brow then pulled her against him, as close as he could get her. "Oh, love, of course I forgive you."

Whenever I balk at following your will, Lord, help me to remember this moment, standing in the snow with her in my arms after so long. I don't want to lose this treasure again.

He pressed a kiss to the top of her head. "Merry Christmas, darling. May I never take your gift of love and forgiveness for granted ever again."

She leaned away from him, giving him a huge smile. "You better not." And then she rose on her tiptoes and pulled him down for a kiss.

He stumbled forward, but in two beats of his heart, he gave up any sense of propriety and drowned himself in the sensation of his wife pouring out a love for him he'd nearly given up on ever feeling again.

She broke their kiss and brought her hand up to his face, swiping at the tears she'd found there. "You're crying."

He swallowed the lump in his throat and nodded, but drew her back to him. Forget tears, he hadn't had enough of her.

After another round of kisses, she pulled away far too soon. "I think we ought to go home."

He gazed at her through the flurry of new snow being unleashed from the heavens. "You're cold?"

Her eyes sparkled. "Not in the slightest."

"Me neither." Could a man die of happiness? "Let's go home."

"To pack?"

He narrowed his eyes at her, and she laughed, shedding the sadness he'd not realized she'd been wearing on her face for ages. His heart lifted so much he couldn't tell if his feet were still on the ground. "I can think of something else I'd rather do than pack. Are we … there yet?"

"That depends on you."

"Oh, good heavens, yes."

She chuckled and laced her arm around his and pulled him toward home.

EPILOGUE

Montana Territory ~ Late Summer, 1885

With the last blow of his hammer, Bryant nailed the final shingle from his stack onto the newly constructed bank. Sitting back on his heels, he wiped the sweat off his forehead with his sleeve. Across the street and down a block, he could make out his daughter in front of City Hall. Only a few books were stacked on the table beside her. Hopefully that meant she'd sold a lot this morning.

To Jennie's right, his wife was engaged in conversation with a plump woman in a pink hat.

"Lunch time!"

Pushing off his knees, he tried not to hobble. He didn't want his boss thinking he was too old to continue roofing. He needed this job until the end of the week.

After climbing down the ladder, Bryant washed up. He wouldn't have long to eat with his family, but he could try to be as presentable as possible.

Dodging the carts in the street, he jogged toward his wife, who'd just finished talking with the lady in pink. Since Jennie was conversing with two other ladies, Bryant took Leah's arm, ignoring her small protest, and pulled her into the alleyway between the city buildings.

"What are you doing?" She laughed. The happy, easy sound was a boon to his heart.

He led her behind a partition, leaned against the wall, and pulled her against him. "I was thinking about last night."

Her eyebrows winged up as she leaned back to look at him. "Oh, you were?"

"Yep." He nuzzled her behind her ear, planting a kiss on her neck. "Want to do that again tonight?"

She shook her head—but not in a manner that meant no. "That'll entirely depend on Jennie turning in early, but she may not. She's sold twelve books so far today!"

"That's wonderful."

"Did you see me talking to the lady in the big pink hat?" Upon his nod, she leaned into him. "She bought Jennie's book at the Christian Church yesterday. Said she read it in one sitting and told all the ladies in her congregation to buy it. They must have listened. We've had a steady stream of customers since nine."

He'd noticed quite a few people, but he'd figured city halls were normally busy. "Good. Let's hope she sells even more so I won't have to lug such a heavy trunk onto the train this Friday."

"Well, enjoy it while it lasts. As soon as we're in Armelle, we're sending in an order for more, maybe even enough to fill two trunks."

He groaned.

"Hey, *I'm* not complaining." She ran a hand down his upper arm. "It's been a long time since you've been this muscular."

He laughed. "Back then, I didn't have to lay on a hot compress at the night just so I could manage to hobble into work the next morning."

"It's getting easier every day. You don't complain too much anymore." She kissed his calloused knuckles. "And with the amount of time that's passed, perhaps someone in Armelle will take a chance and hire you—for labor, anyway."

"Speaking of home, I went by the post office earlier." He pulled out the letter he'd tried not to wrinkle all morning.

Leah stiffened. "From Ava? Is everything all right? Don't tell me she had the baby early and we missed it, or—" She put her hand to her throat and her face drained of color.

"Nothing bad has happened. You worry too much." He slipped the cabinet card from the envelope and glanced at Lenora's impish grin, matched by the mischievous glint in her eyes as she held onto a little rocking chair. "Our grandbaby's got will power. She stood still long enough that only her hands are blurred."

"Exactly like her mother—sassy and stubborn." Leah took the picture and gazed at it lovingly. "But why send this now? They know we're on our way back."

"I think she was just eager to show off the picture." He unfolded Ava's letter and pointed to a section for Leah to read. "But this is why she wrote."

As she skimmed, her forehead wrinkled adorably. The scar running through her brow begged him to press his lips against it, as he did whenever he noted the permanent mark of his selfishness stamped upon her face. How unworthy and blessed he was to still have this woman in his arms.

Leah's eyes widened suddenly. "The McGills are going to let us stay at their place?"

"Seems so. That'll keep us from crowding Ava and Oliver."

Leah pressed the letter against her chest and stared at the brick wall opposite them. "Do you think your staying there will ruin the hard work Bo's put in to restoring their family name?"

He frowned. He'd not thought of that. Leah's steady love and Jennie's dependence often made him forget that a cloud still hung over his head. "Maybe we should decline their invitation —or at least, I should. I can bunk at Jake's or Nolan's. You're the one Ava needs anyway."

"Ah, but I need you." She turned in his arms and framed his face with her hands. "And you'll be handy for keeping Lenora entertained while we wash diapers and burp the little one."

"I'd hoped Oliver would do that. Maybe if I'm not there, he'll have to."

She unfolded the letter, probably to read it from the beginning. "Let's not dismiss the offer right away. Perhaps Ava knows how people will react to you better than we do—we have been gone nearly eight months."

"I don't know…"

She gave him a sly half-smile on her face. "If I'm going to be sleeping in the fanciest room I've ever stayed in…" She planted a soft, lingering kiss by the corner of his mouth. "I'll want you with me."

His heart never failed to trip when she whispered such things to him. He leaned his forehead against hers. "I do love sharing a room with you."

She laughed and pushed him away slightly, her eyes glittering. "That's no secret."

He leaned down to kiss her, but the unfinished letter seemed to be warring for her attention. He broke away with one last light peck on her lips so she could read through the rest of the letter.

When she finished, she lowered her hand, letting the letter hang at her side. "I'm surprised the McGills would be so generous. I mean, why us?"

"You've always said Gwen wasn't as bad as people thought, and from what you and Jake told me, Bo's worked hard to make up for what his father did, so apples *can* fall far from the tree. I hope ours don't though. Our girls would be lucky to turn out exactly like you."

She sighed as she flipped the letter over. "If only Oliver were more like you."

He shook his head, knowing the only thing in that letter that could be considered as Ava speaking ill of Oliver was how much time he'd spent building a larger root cellar. "He's not an ex-convict, which completely makes up for any lack of attention on his part."

Leah whirled about and gave him the look she used to give the girls when they were naughty. "Oliver and I and everyone else in this world are no better than you in light of God's law. No one's perfect. But thank God, no matter how badly we do, He loves us still—just as I love you."

He smoothed back a strand of her hair that had fallen over her brow. "You've always been too good for me, you know that?"

"No, it's God who's good."

"You're right." He soaked in the sight of one of the most precious gifts God had ever given him, then pressed a kiss against her hairline. "He's been so very good."

I hope you enjoyed *Depending on You*!

If you did, please take a moment to share with others. You can do so by posting an honest review wherever you purchased this book and also on social media. Every review and mention helps!

To keep up with the latest news about my books, please make sure you're on my newsletter list at melissajagears.com

More stories in the *Frontier Vows* series are being written. In the meantime, if you'd like to read Jacob and Annie's or Nolan and Corinne's romance, check out *Romancing the Bride* and *Pretending to Wed*. If you've already read those, I have a free story to hold you off in the meantime, check out *Love by the Letter: A Novella* which starts my *Unexpected Brides* series.

AUTHOR'S NOTE

For those curious about the historicity of Jennie's self-publishing ventures, I wanted to write a bit about what I learned about the blind at this time in history. Blind children were often babied and sheltered by parents who were at a loss at how to help them. When blind schools came along, many were shocked at how well the people they'd relegated to the sidelines could learn. Schools gave the blind confidence in themselves and lifted their spirits with activity and education which had been previously denied them; however, upon leaving the schools, the blind often struggled to survive in the workplace. Many begged to return to the schools and work for room and board.

Once these schools realized education alone wasn't enough, many set up shops to help their alumni stay out of the poor houses.

Those who ran the blind schools worked hard to advocate on behalf of their students, but soon, many of those students became their own advocates through writing. Some chose to self-publish their stories and peddle them to support themselves and inform the public that they were more than their disability. Jennie's plan is modeled on those entrepreneurs who were desperate to provide for themselves and eager to enlighten the sighted.

If you'd like to learn more about what the blind faced in the 1800s, I'd suggest reading the article, "The Meanings of Blindness in Nineteenth-Century America" by Ernest Freeburg. If you use Google, you should be able to find a link to the pdf through AmericanAntiquarian.org in the search results.

ACKNOWLEDGMENTS

Stories beg to be told, but never start out perfect. Thanks to Heidi Chiavaroli, Myra Johnson, Natalie Monk, and Naomi Rawlings for their skilled insight and fitting me into their busy lives to help me craft this story into something more enjoyable for readers. Thanks to my beta readers for catching the little things: Sarah Keimig, Stephanie McCall, Amy Parker, and Anne-Marie Turenne. And to Judy DeVries for proofreading and Najla Qamber for the beautiful cover.

Also, thanks to my husband and children, who love me in spite of myself. I, like Bryant, have been given a gift I didn't deserve when God gave me all of you.

ABOUT THE AUTHOR

Much to her introverted self's delight, award-winning writer Melissa Jagears hardly needs to leave home to be a home-schooling mother and novelist. She lives in Kansas with her husband and three children and can be found online at Facebook, BookBub, Pinterest, Goodreads, and melissajagears.com. Feel free to drop her a note at author@melissajagears.com, or you can find her current mailing address and an updated list of her books on her website.

To keep up to date with Melissa's news and book releases, subscribe to her newsletter at melissajagears.com

facebook.com/melissajagearsauthor

twitter.com/MelissaJagears

pinterest.com/melissajagears

goodreads.com/Melissa_Jagears

bookbub.com/authors/melissa-jagears

amazon.com/author/melissajagears

Published by Utmost Publishing
www.utmostpublishing.com

Printed in the United States of America

Publisher's Cataloging-in-Publication Data

Names: Jagears, Melissa.
   Title: Depending on you / Melissa Jagears
   Description: Wichita, KS: Utmost Pub., 2020. | Series: Frontier Vows
   Identifiers: LCCN 2020921877 | ISBN 9781948678087 (pbk.) | ISBN 9781948678070 (ebk.)

Scripture quotations are from the King James Version of the Bible.

Cover design © Qamber Designs and Media
   Author represented by Natasha Kern Literary Agency

Made in United States
North Haven, CT
21 January 2022

15055673R00074